The Emperor's Railroad

Also by Guy Haley

THE
EMPEROR'S
RAILROAD

───── A TALE OF THE DREAMING CITIES ─────

GUY HALEY

A TOM DOHERTY ASSOCIATES BOOK

NEW YORK

This is a work of fiction. All of the characters, organization, and events portrayed in this novella are either products of the author's imagination or are used fictitiously.

THE EMPEROR'S RAILROAD

Cover art by Chris McGrath
Cover designed by Christine Foltzer

Edited by Lee Harris

A Tor.com Book
Published by Tom Doherty Associates, LLC
175 Fifth Avenue
New York, NY 10010

www.tor.com

Tor® is a registered trademark of Tom Doherty Associates, LLC.

ISBN 978-1-4668-9197-5 (ebook)
ISBN 978-0-7653-8984-8 (trade paperback)

First Edition: April 2016

Bridge of the Ancients

QUINN HAD TWO SWORDS. One for killing the living, and one for killing the dead.

He wore them on top of each other on his left hip. On his right he had a six-gun.

A knight's weapons.

You've probably not seen a knight. There's not been one through these parts for a long time, not since just after Quinn, and that was fifty years back. Back then I'd never seen one neither. Truth be told, when we first saw him we weren't right sure if he was what he said he was. There weren't many knights left in those days; most had fallen in the war. Times like these we live in, you wonder at people. A knight's weapons are hard to get hold of if you ain't sanctioned by the Dreaming Cities, but not impossible.

My mom, she had her suspicions. But I knew from the start that he was a good man, I swear.

So this here's the story of how I met Quinn, a knight of the angels. As it happens, it's also the story of how I ended up here in the Winfort, and got involved with a dragon along the way.

First I got to say this. Time goes, it rubs away at your memory sure as the Kanawha River rubs at its banks. Memory moves. The river is still there, but the course is different, do you understand? I'm telling you this story, and I've told it before. Maybe it changes a bit every time I tell it, even when I'm sure that's *exactly* what happened and it couldn't be no other way. This is a wise thing, pay attention.

It's the way people are. You never been in a heated argument that your recollection is right and that of your friend or brother is wrong? That's how bad people are at remembering truly. The words my mom said to me on our journey that I'm going to tell you, they sure as hell ain't the exact same words she used. Things happened that I forget, things happened that I remember a bit different every time I bring them to mind. Bits get dreamed up to join up the parts I do remember. And I'm getting older. Real old. My mind ain't what it was. I open my eyes and everything is colored gray. I close them and it looks like the past is drenched in gold. The future is ashes, the past is treasure, seems to me, but do you think that's really how it is? I'm not far from dead, is all. When you get where I am, I'm sure the past'll look brighter to you as well.

Memory. Biggest traitor there is.

You get others involved, telling their memories of my memories, well, when I'm gone and you tell this story to someone else, then it'll change some more. That's how memories become stories, and everyone with a lick of sense knows stories ain't the truth.

Saying that, there are some few things that never change, no matter how many times you think on them. Jewels in a box, you take them out from time to time to look at them and they never change. Some things stick in the mind unchanged forever. There were a lot of times like that on our journey.

One of them was seeing Quinn fight the first time on the edge of the Kanawha River, at the Emperor's Railroad bridge. If I close my eyes, I see it clearer than I can see now, like I'm there again and seeing it for the first time.

This is how it is: my mom's got her arms around my neck, like that'd protect me from the dead and they'd not just rip me from her. The sun is warm, but the morning cold, like they get to be in fall. The trees are got up in their finery, yellows, reds, and oranges. A Virginian morning, a late October morning. My mom's heart's beating so hard behind my head. I'm twelve, not long that age and afraid I'll not see thirteen. She is scared. I'm scared. But there's no shame in fear, not at a time like this.

That's what it's like. It's happening in my mind right now.

There was the roar of the rapids downriver, water pouring over the leavings of the Gone Before. The moans of the dead. Quinn's weapons hacking into flesh, meaty and workmanlike, not like I imagined a knight's blade craft should be. Sight, sound; but the smells are the most important. That's when you can tell it's a true memory. I can smell the soap and the light tang of sweat on my mother, the road dirt and the leaf mold from camping in the woods. The weedy smell of the river, heavy and round. The smell at our backs of Quinn's horses. Quinn himself, strong sweat, but clean and sharp, almost like lemons. Leather and iron.

And the stink of the dead. That ripe, rank stink, the shit on their hindquarters, old blood, vomit. All the hidden nastiness of the human body worn on the outside. They're the devil's affront to God.

The railroad bridge wasn't like it is now, with the trains coming over four times a week. This here is still wild country, but it was wilder then. The new bridge is big, but you got to imagine what it was in the Gone Before. In those days it didn't have a deck of wood for the trains, but a wide road of concrete for their miraculous carriages, tens of feet wide, and a road on that so smooth you could roll a marble clear from one end to the other with a little flick of your finger. That had mostly gone into the river by the time I saw it. But the piers stayed sound.

That's why the old emperor had chosen it for his railroad, laying a new bridge over the old piers. Back then it was the only way across the Kanawha north of Charleston. Still is.

The dead came out of the trees as we'd come up to it. Eight of them, hop-scrambling towards us, arms out, hands grasping. They don't have no sense; they started moaning as soon as they smelled us, and Quinn had his heavy sword out before they were up the bank. If they'd waited, showed a bit of cunning, we'd have come off a lot worse. But the dead aren't people no more. One lunged up out of the brush, ripping a nasty gash down the shoulder of Quinn's big white horse. Quinn chopped down, spilling its rotten brains on the grass. The others were a ways off, staggering up from the nearer the water.

"Watch the horses," he said. He never shouted, and he was never scared. He slid off his horse—Parsifal it was called—and walked into the dead. He didn't charge, or yell. He walked down to them calmly, then set to cutting them down like he was reaping wheat.

We didn't have no weapons. Simple folks like us are forbidden the likes of what Quinn had, sharp steel and gunpowder. The dead lunged at him, clacking their teeth, raking at him with their fingernails.

These dead ones were hungry. There'd not been many folk up this way since the emperor's fall, what few there were were right here in the Winfort and did not venture as far south as the river.

With nothing to eat, the dead had chewed their own lips off. Their teeth were long and brown. Clotted blood was thick round their chins and on their chests. I hate the teeth the worst, I seen too much ill come from teeth like that. You watch me next mealtime, you'll see I can't be looking at anyone's face, in case they forget their manners and chew with their mouths open. Makes me sick because it makes me think on the unliving.

The dead were naked. When they're long gone over like that the clothes rot off or get torn away. Not a stitch on them. The nakedness makes them worse, somehow, makes them seem more human rather than less. I've seen men that reckon themselves brave turn and run at the sight of a pack like that. Not Quinn. I knew for sure he was a knight then, right at that moment, badge or not.

One of them got a hold of him, made my mom gasp out over and over, "Oh God, oh sweet dear Jesus." Mom wasn't one for blaspheming. That made it twice in one week, the other time being when Walter died. It never was a habit with her.

Fingers thin as twigs but strong as roots wrapped themselves round the top of Quinn's off arm. An unliving's head lunged for his bicep. It couldn't bite through Quinn's mail, but it didn't let up, gnawing on his arm like a hungry man on a cob of corn, blood pouring out of its gums. Quinn let it break its teeth on his armor, and buried his sword in the head of another.

His heavy sword, the dead-killing sword, he called that a falchion. Quinn had lots of fancy words for things; for bits of his armor, for the past, for what he'd done, but he did it in that sort of way that made me think he was laughing at himself. This is a tasset, he'd say, this a pauldron, this is a falchion. The falchion was like the machetes we use to cut back the brush and clear a field, but heavier and longer, because his falchion was for the kind of weed that bites back.

The man-killing sword was lighter, four feet long. Straight where the falchion was curved, a fancy basket round the hilt that shone so bright I was sure it was silver, not steel.

That longsword stayed in its sheath most of the time. He wore his swords atop each other, and the hilts knocked together sometimes when he walked. When that happened, his hand went down, did this little motion to reset them so they wouldn't tangle when he drew. He did it without thinking. It was a movement he must've done a million times before. His gun he wore on his right hip, because it's different pulling a gun to a sword. Gun goes up, swords across. I only saw him use his gun the once.

We'll get to that.

Quinn cut the dead man diagonally between the eyes. The skull made hollow noise, like a gourd split with a big knife. The dead man's eyes rolled up in his head, and he died a second time. Quinn wrenched his falchion free. The other unliving was still at his arm, stumps of his teeth grinding themselves away on the mail. Quinn caved in its skull with three blows from his pommel. This was mighty big; a falchion's got a heavy blade, and needs balancing.

That left five of the unliving, shambling in that way they have. Two were pawing at him, the other three still coming on, slowly. Their ribs were all showing in their skin, arms like sticks. They didn't have it in them to run. They were starved.

Quinn cut down both by him. One lost its head, the other the use of its legs. Then he marched up to the others, bold as you like. The first one lost its hand to his sword, then its brains. Quinn was away to slam the second down with his left arm. The thing drops, and he steps over it, killing the last one with a single chop that took his blade clean down through its shoulder, most of the way to the heart. Then he pivoted on the spot, smooth as a cat, and cut the head right from the neck of the one he'd slammed down as it tried to get up.

He pulled off his helmet as he walked back to us, then the leather breathing mask under it. "Curse on the air, you ain't got a care, curse in the mouth, you're headed south." You know the rhyme. You got to get bit, or get a lot of blood in you, to turn. Quinn wasn't taking any chances. He said he always wore his mask under his helmet when he was fighting the dead. He pulled out raw cotton pads from pouches in the breathing mask and threw them away. He was sweating, but he wasn't panting. He wasn't even out of breath.

He checked around the dead. The one that he'd cut the legs out from moaned and scraped at the floor, the bones shiny white in the wounds. Thick blood pumped from the cuts, each spurt showing less vigor.

"You okay?" Quinn said. He didn't say much, and what he did say was quiet.

My mom nodded. "Yes, yes. Thank you." Her voice was breathy. She hugged me closer.

I looked at him. I was awestruck. "You *are* a knight," I said. I was raised on stories of his kind. He was a hero to me.

He looked down at me, his expression unreadable. He had leathery skin, eyes narrowed by looking into the sun too much, a thick brown beard shot with gray. What I thought of as an old man's face, and by that I meant he looked forty, forty-five maybe. He wasn't like any man I'd seen. He was pale, really pale, and when he opened his eyes up, they were round. Not narrow like with other folks. Knights are all funny looking, you ask me. Not long after Quinn I saw two more knights coming through here, one with skin so dark it was near black, another one like Quinn, only paler yet, and with bright red hair. That's a story for another day. The point I'm driving at here is that knights are surely people, but they look different than you or me.

I asked him once how old he was. "Older than you," he said. That was that.

My mom tugged me in her arms, a hug with a rebuke in it. "Forgive my son, sir." I was pretty sure she doubted he was a knight still.

"He's a boy," said Quinn, as if that explained something. He went to his horses. He had two. Parsifal was a tall, powerful stallion. He warned us against surprising it, but he let Mom and me ride it while he walked. The other horse was a round little pony that carried his gear. Clemente, he called it. Clemente took two strides for every one of the stallion's, but it never tired. Both of them were cropping grass, neither bothered by the blood and stink. Quinn went to his charger and checked its wound. Shallow scratches, it turned out.

"Is he going to die?" I said.

"It looks worse than it is," said Quinn. It did look bad, three parallel grooves, deep and bright with blood. He pulled out a fingernail from the bottom of one and threw it aside. That's how strong the dead can be, strong enough to tear through horse hide. They rip their own fingernails out, and they don't feel a damn thing.

He cleaned out the wound with a rag and something that smelled like moonshine.

"Why's he doing that, Mom?" I asked.

"Infection, got to clean it," said Quinn. "The animals don't get the sickness, but they incubate it. And those things can give you a bad case of blood poisoning even if you don't get what they've got."

There was a moan from the dead on the ground. I started and clutched at my mom's sleeve.

"Mr. Quinn . . ." my mom began.

"That dead ain't dead! You gotta kill it, mister."

Quinn glanced at the dead man, slowly bleeding his way to his second death. Quinn went back to cleaning out the scratch on his horse's shoulder.

"They aren't dead, kid, they just seem that way. That one won't last long. He'll die soon enough. Takes longer for them to die than a healthy man, but a wound that will kill you will kill them. Eventually."

Half the time Quinn spoke like regular folks. But the other half he spoke strangely, old-fashioned like; you might say educated. My mother wasn't a poor woman, not to start with. She had some learning, and she passed it on to me. Some of the children at New Karlsville used to tease me for it. Mom said they were afraid of what I knew and they didn't. They had to slap me down to make themselves feel better, that they were stronger in their ignorance. I still know a few things that some don't, and that ain't all down to the teachings of the Lord. But Quinn, the way he spoke made me sound like the worst kind of wildman from the deepest woods, the ones that think giants built the world Gone Before, and sacrifice their kids to the angels. And the things he knew . . .

"How can you be sure, sir?"

"Are you afraid of blood, kid?"

"No, sir!" I shook my head hard.

"Then go see for yourself. It won't have the strength to hurt you. It will bleed out in a few minutes."

"Why don't you just kill it?" I didn't like the moaning, but I wasn't going to say that.

"I won't risk the edge on my blade. Hacking down at the ground'll blunt it."

"Show some pity, Mr. Quinn!" said my mom. She had a way about her, she was used to people doing what she said.

"Why?" he said, not looking at her. "It can't feel anything. The mind's all gone from that one. There's no man in there. There's nothing but animal left."

She took in a deep breath, and tried again. "Could you show a little mercy, please, for the sake of my son?

You say you are a knight, you should behave like one in front of him." I pulled away from my mom then. She was angry and didn't notice. "That poor man was once like you or I. He deserves a little dignity. Is there not something in your code of honor, sir?"

Quinn shrugged, and carried on cleaning out his horse's cut.

By that point, I was over by the dead man.

Mom noticed where I'd gotten to and cried out. "Abney! Stay away!" Sometimes she could get a bit shrill, overprotective, I felt. I was that age where I always knew better. I didn't pay her no attention.

The dead man was on the floor, his head rolling back and forth. I was fascinated and repulsed. I couldn't look away from it. Quinn's cut had smashed the bones in both thighs as well as cutting them deep. That's how heavy a weapon a falchion is. It couldn't move. It looked at me hungrily with those pale blue eyes they all have. Its mouth and nose were bloody holes. A black tongue, sore with self-inflicted bites, ran over its teeth. I hate the teeth.

Quinn shoved me back. His leather glove was rough on my chest, even through my shirt. He had his falchion in his hand.

"Not *that* close," he said.

Although it's a heavy sword meant for chopping, a falchion does have a point. Carefully, Quinn put this against the dead man's left eye. The dead man groped at Quinn's legs, but Quinn paid it no mind. He leaned on his sword pommel with both hands, pushing the point down through the skull. There was a scraping noise and a crack of bone. A slow breath escaped the dead man's lips, the sigh of a man sinking into exhaustion after a hard day in the fields, and he was still.

"Dead now," Quinn said.

Another rag came out. He wiped his sword with it. The rag went into a different pouch to the one it had come out of. Then he held the weapon up in line with his eyes, sighted down the blade for nicks, then slid the sword back into its scabbard. Then he checked his shoulder and his hands, not so much for bites to his flesh, I think, but for damage to his armor. The leather and steel were filthy with the blood of the unliving, but otherwise unmarked. "Going to take a while to clean this off," he said.

"We do not have the luxury—" began my mother.

"I didn't mean now." He looked down at the rushes between the bank and the first pier. The old road approaching the bridge had been raised up on some sort of causeway; where it had sagged it'd been filled in with rubble and spoil by the emperor's men for their railroad, but that had been twenty years back. The repairs were beginning to fail. The emperor's engineers did not have the skill of the Gone Before. Trees were growing up between the sleepers. In one place the bank had been washed out, leaving rusty iron rails hanging over nothing.

From the embankment to the bridge's first pier was a wide gap in the old road, it having fallen in the Good Lord alone knows when. Being close to the river like that kept the rubble free of dirt, so we could see the worn slabs of it draped broke-backed over the bank and stretch of water. Thick ivy clogged the pier's upper part. A gust of wind made the leaves rattle, passing on to ripple the brown river with silver waves. Any sound in a place like that can make you startle, and I did.

The old bridge had been made out of concrete, the molding stone of the Gone Before, the new bridge from wood and iron. The emperor's bridge had been made on a grand scale by the standards of this diminished era. It was wide enough for a train, with good, broad walkways for the draft horses on both sides.

All this was carried up on a big old latticework of huge wooden beams. These were arranged in squares ten feet by ten feet, with a diagonal brace across each, all tied up with iron. It looked real impressive, but twenty cold Virginian winters and twenty humid Virginian summers do a lot of damage. The beams were the kind of wet that don't dry easy, the wood splintery, rotted right through in places. Moss clung to every surface not directly in the wind. It being that time of year there were about ten kinds of fungus on it. Vines and briars trailed off into the water. The iron of the rails and the ties was bright orange, and streaked the wood. We looked nervously at it, but this was the only way to get to Cousin Matthew up at the Winfort, so we were crossing it, happily or not.

"Wait here," Quinn said. He went down the bank, picking his way through the wooden supports of the emperor's bridge, right down to where the water was pale with fallen rubble and the river foamed over the weirs they made. There were concrete caves with flat roofs there, and he checked them for more dead. A duck burst from the water's edge twenty yards downriver. Wings clattering, it blared an angry alarm. An uneasy silence followed. Quinn came back. He breathed out one long, thoughtful exhalation, and scanned the banks with those wrinkled-in eyes of his. I don't know what he saw. I couldn't see anything but woods and reeds and the Emperor's Railroad.

"We'll not cross all the way tonight," he said.

"You have changed your mind?" my mother said.

"Dead slowed us down. There's an hour of daylight left, not enough to find us a good campground," he said. He was so sure of everything he said. When he said there was an hour of daylight, well, that's what there would be, pretty much exactly. "It's twenty miles further to Winfort. We have to cross slowly, the wood's rotted all to hell and the emperor never did build as good as he boasted. By the time we're over, it'll be dark. We'll camp on the middle section, where the road from the Gone Before stands." He pointed to the middle, one of two points where concrete deck still stood. The other being just across from us between the first and second piers. The railroad had been laid directly onto the old deck in those parts. "We'll finish the crossing tomorrow. We'd be better trying to get all the way to Winfort in one day anyhow."

"What about the bandits?" my mom said. "You've had us near running through these woods, Mr. Quinn, for fear of them. Are you not worried by them any longer?"

Quinn shrugged. "Not as worried as I am by the dead," he said. "These are old, long turned, and near starved. But where there is one pack, there're always more. In the middle we can see anyone coming, living or dead."

"And they, Mr. Quinn, will be able to see us!"

Quinn's jaw set. "Truth is, ma'am, we are not going much further tonight. Last thing I'm wanting to do is come down on the far side of the river when night's drawing in. The dragon'll be most active then. I took on your employment on the understanding you'd do what I said. These are dangerous lands."

"You said they weren't dead, mister," I blurted. I felt

the tension rising between the adults. I had to say something on my mother's side. I was the man of the family, at least for a day or so more until we got to Winfort. There was a contradiction in what Quinn said, one I could understand. I seized on it.

Quinn gave me a quirk-mouthed look, the kind that tells you you're being dumb.

"How can you be sure?" my mother asked. She was a pretty woman, even when she was stern. She commanded a high bride price for it. I didn't understand all the business of matrimony back when I was a boy. Not until I got older did I look back and understand what I'd seen. When she and my stepfather Gern were going through the endless step and counterstep of the marriage dance with each other, I wondered if he'd been blinded by her prettiness, thinking she had no brains to match. He found alright that she had plenty. My mom was not a woman to take orders from anyone, least of all a man.

Still, that was all done. Gern was dead, along with everyone else in New Karlsville. All we had of Gern was the bride price she'd saved all them years, and she'd promised a deal of that to Quinn.

"I'm sure, ma'am," said Quinn. He never looked at my mother when he spoke to her. There was that reserve to him, more than him simply being formal. "If you don't like what I say, stay here."

"That is not our agreement."

"Well then," said Quinn, as if that settled it. He went for his horses. "You first. This bridge'll bear you better than my horses."

By way of comment on his judgment, the emperor's bridge creaked.

"Wind's picking up." He sniffed the air. "We best be on our way."

~

I didn't like the look of the bridge. My mother didn't like the look of it either, although she hid it better than me. She took a breath to steady her nerves, sort of a high sound that was too long for a gasp, too short for a sigh.

Mom went first, up by the left-hand edge where she could grab the vertical beams for support. Someone had tacked up a rope there for a handrail sometime, but whenever it was it was long ago, and the rope was rotten gray where it wasn't green. Mom told me not to touch it.

"Put your feet here, at the edges," she said, placing her own where the beams were fixed into the side. She crept forward, putting her feet carefully one directly in front of the other. "Not this one, Abney," she'd say. "Go careful here," and so on. All while she moved forward resolutely. She had her mouth set in that thin line that said she was taking no nonsense, not from old Garrett down the store or from the sheriffs, or from any damn bridge. I don't reckon I've met any man as brave as my mother.

"Now you," said Quinn quietly, when Mom was halfway.

I stepped up to the brink. The first beam was missing, the second a worrying dark brown and slick with it. Through the gap I could see the ground, only a few feet below me where the bridge rose up, but the bank dropped away frighteningly fast. I took a deep breath and stepped forward. I did just what my mom had done, one foot in front of the other, right at the place where the beams joined into the sides of the bridge. It wasn't so bad to begin with, but as the bridge got higher and higher my breath came a little harder, a little sharper. My eyes shifted from my hands to my feet the whole time. Frightened I'd grab at a rotten piece of wood or rope, then frightened I'd put my foot through a hole I didn't see coming because I was so busy looking at where I should put my hands. I got scared, and went quicker.

"Slow down, Abney!" my mother warned.

I wanted to be brave, for my mom, but I didn't slow down. I stopped.

My mom was standing on the old road on the first pier. Jagged gums of concrete with rusty holes showing where iron teeth had been. She gave me that wide-eyed stare mothers do when they're mad at you but don't want to shout because they're scared for you too.

My eyes skated down, between my feet. Between the gaps in the wood I saw rushes, the black blood of the dead, green lazy waters. I imagined falling right through that rotten old wood and plunging under the surface, never to be seen again.

I froze. Mr. Quinn cleared his throat. I turned my head. There he was, waiting patient as you like, holding the reins of that big horse and little pony of his.

There was no fear in him, like he wasn't going to take a ton of horseflesh out over a rotten-wood bridge. His armor was dirty, the leather of his belts and scabbards and holsters were dusty and cracked. His beard and hair were wild. But he was still a knight, and I looked like a fool in front of him.

That embarrassment was enough to send me over to the far side. I scampered across the last part. My mom put her hand on my shoulder. She searched my eyes for a moment, one hand under my chin to tilt my face up. Then her face wrinkled with concern for Quinn.

Quinn led his stallion over, all nonchalant like. One hand on the reins, the other lightly on the supports at the side. The horse kept its head down, hooves picking out the good wood. Quinn joined us, passed one rein to my mother without a word. The horse bent his big white head and started crunching on the grass growing on the ancient deck. Rip, crunch crunch, that way horses do. I ain't never heard anything make so big a meal out of grass as a horse. You ever notice that?

That horse was so clean and white and Quinn so dirty you'd think Quinn had stolen it from a better man. Its harness was well-oiled and its coat shone. Every night, after we set camp, before he ate, he fed his beasts and he oiled the leather. Every night. He curried the pair of them for a half hour before the last light went, then worked their coats with soft brushes. When we first saw him, a vagabond on a knight's horse . . . Well, you can't blame us for getting the wrong idea. I ain't ashamed to admit it. But we had to trust him. We had no choice. Good luck for us he was what he said, and not what he seemed.

Quinn ran back down the bridge. His pony came less surely than his riding horse, but it came anyways. Halfway across that time a beam snapped, not loud; a soft wet crack, like a bone going. My mom's hand was up to her mouth, her other gripped the front of my jacket. She pulled me in so close she knocked my hat forward and I wriggled to get some space. I had to see what would happen.

Nothing did happen to Quinn, not ever. The beam bent, but did not give, and he got across.

~

The bridge was a large reminder of the works of the Gone Before, a strong, massive thing that no man for a hundred miles of this place has any idea how to build, and no man a thousand miles past that has the things he needs to get it done. Long and straight, the bridge had lasted out the years since the Fall when so many others had collapsed entirely. But there ain't no thing in this world so mighty as time, and so the bridge was going the way of all things: finally, slowly sinking into ruinous grandeur. Great girders of steel had held it high. This part of the country had been empty for a long time, and there was so much metal in easier spots that no one had gotten round to scavenging it. Most of the iron that had been there come the Fall was still there come our journey, rusted paper thin by years of rain, twisted by the sagging of the road they held, but still there, shaggy in coats of ivy. In sheltered spots the rust was worst, often rotted right through. But sometimes—around rivets big as your fist, in the corners where the metal had been joined by the Gone Before—you could see spots of ancient paint.

We are iron, the girders said to me. You cannot bring us low. They were wrong about that. They were warped and fallen as the men who'd made them, broken as a spiderweb poked with a stick, but they were going down fighting. You got to respect that.

There were four piers all told. The road had been wide, big enough for four wagons, I reckon. At the southern and northern parts, between the first and second pier and the third and the fourth, the deck still stood over the water. The emperor had shored up the original structure there so that his railroad could run over it. The section in the middle was soon to give up the ghost. The road hung from piers at one side only, the other half sloping almost into the water. But it was safe to cross if you stuck to the high upstream side; the rest was a treacherous slope of cracked concrete full of bushes, trees, and poison ivy that ran all the way into the water. That part went in years back, way before King Jonas rebuilt the bridge properly, but when we crossed it was still hanging in there.

Between the bank and the first pier, between the fourth pier and the bank, all the old deck was in the water. The emperor's flimsy wooden parasite crossed the gaps. Down in the river, trailing weed, were the works of mightier men.

What concrete was left was full of holes, cracked by the weather and roots. Trees grew all over it. The bridge wasn't a bridge anymore, but an island floating in the sky. Quinn brought his horses along, nice and slow, always looking for broken iron or holes that might catch their feet and break their legs.

"Why'd they need such big roads?" I said. The Emperor's Railroad looked pathetic on the bridge.

"There were a lot more people than there are now," Quinn said.

"God took it away, Abney," Mom said.

Quinn shook his head. "They threw it away, is what happened."

My mother was a god-fearing woman. She frowned at me, her way of telling me Quinn was wrong.

Downriver were the rapids. A bunch of low, crumbling islands stuck up out of the water, too regular to be natural. More work from the Gone Before. Those islands stop the river up good there. All those bridges down the rivers foul up the water for us. You can't take anything down that stretch with a draft of more than a yard or so, the trash in there'd tear the bottom right out of it. That hundred-foot length of rapids are the reason you can't take a boat to the Ohio River, and all the trade from Charleston has to get from the Kanawha to the Ohio by way of the railroad out to Huntingdon docks.

There was some talk about the emperor digging a canal, opening up the way from Charlotte to the Ohio once his war was over. But he offended the Lord, the sickness came back, the dragon came, and that was that. These days the king is talking on it. Things never change.

You only got an idea of what the Gone Before might have been like from up high. I could see the lines of the streets and the roads in the patterns of the trees, those marshes and forests that had been the homes of men. Now they're only irregularities in the patterns of God's world. I wondered then, and I've wondered many times since, how long before those traces are eaten up, broken down by the plants, pulled to pieces and digested by the Earth, so that there's nothing left at all.

We reached the last stretch of sound concrete. Here a section of wooden bridge stretched out down to the northern bank, as rotten as and streaked with rust off the railroad as the southern section. In the dark it looked pathetic compared to the structure it sat atop of—a phantom of a bridge. There was an overgrown clearing at the end studded with tumbledown walls, swampy land beyond.

"We'll stop here," Quinn said.

So we camped on the flying island. Did they have real floating islands, back then in the Gone Before? I've heard it said they could do most anything.

We were in a tight spot. Dead men in the woods, something worse beyond, and we had to go through to get to a cousin Mom wasn't even sure was still alive. I must have looked scared, because my mom pulled me close and murmured, "No one can get up here, not without Quinn seeing, don't you worry."

I couldn't help but think that whatever might happen there, it couldn't be as bad as what had happened to New Karlsville.

The Road to Charleston

I HAVEN'T TOLD YOU how we met Quinn yet.

Here's how it went. Three days before we crossed the bridge, the axle on Walter's mail wagon broke, and he fell. And because he fell, he died. Walter's end was a stupid, pointless one, brought on by a pothole. One moment he was laughing—that moustache of his bristling like a catfish's whiskers—then there was a bang, a crack, a lurch, his hand went out for support, found none. My mom swiped for his fingers but missed, and he toppled off the seat. A wet bang as his skull connected with a rock, placed just right to catch him on the head. Almost malicious, like it was done on purpose. We were sad for his loss; of all the people that could have helped us after New Karlsville fell, only he did.

When we scrambled off the mail wagon into the road he wasn't moving. My mother turned him over. His eyes were staring at nothing. There was a perfect round dent in his head big enough for half a cup of flour. But he was still breathing. We did what we could, which wasn't much, and he died.

Mom made sure he didn't come back. She was never squeamish about that.

For the second time in a month we were waiting to see what God had in store for us. The road was one from the Gone Before. I'll tell you how you can tell their roads. The surface they used is gone. But earthworks, they stay put until shifted. You see a long, long dip, like a big ditch or a dry river, with embankments that don't seem to serve no useful purpose? Chances are it's an old road. This one had been broad enough to build a house across, a big house at that, now it was barely more than a track. Trees and scrub had encroached on its width from the sides and from the middle. Sometimes you'd catch sight of broken things from the time before. Most often bridges, where one of their roads crossed another. In New Karlsville we used to call them from the Gone Before "Bridge Builders," they made so many.

The state of the road tells you a lot about how important New Karlsville was. But sorry though it was, the road was a main way to Charleston from the south, so we were hopeful someone would be along, and that they wouldn't be a man with a black heart.

"The Good Lord provides," my mom said. She said that a lot.

I couldn't keep my eyes off the trees. Dense forest round there, where we was, and not a sign of civilized human life.

We were four hours there before Quinn rode up. We heard his horses' hooves thumping hollowly on the mulch first, and his gear jangling. We looked down the road. He appeared round a corner, his horses' feet ringing louder as he crossed onto the small patch of bare concrete we were sitting on. My mother drew up her knees, stared resolutely at him. She was afraid of this man with his gun and his swords.

Quinn—we didn't know his name then—Quinn glanced at our wagon sagging on its broken axle, then he looked not at us exactly, more over our heads. He rarely looked you in the eye. Often when he did look a man in the eye, it meant trouble.

I'm not a liar, so I'm not going to say when he came riding up to us that first day that we didn't think he might be a thief. The suspicion lingered, days after he took us on, until that time when I saw Quinn fight. Then I knew for sure he was what he said he was.

"Dangerous country this," said the man who might have been a knight, or might have been a murderer.

My mother did not reply.

"Where are you headed?" he said.

"North," said my mother. Her voice was unusually clipped, dismissive. She wanted him to pass on by.

"Charleston?" he said.

My mother said nothing.

"Further?" he said.

My mother nodded, just slightly.

"Where?"

No reply.

"I don't mean any harm."

She looked at him, openly hostile.

"I can help you, ma'am."

"It is not your concern where we are headed, sir," my mother said.

Quinn shifted on his saddle. "Okay." He said nothing for a minute. His horse snorted and paced from foot to foot, impatient to be on. His pack pony was already cropping grass. Quinn looked at the wagon. "Not safe, a boy and a woman alone. I'm headed north. I'll take you to Charleston."

"Your weapons, your armor. They are those of a knight," my mother said.

"They are," he said.

"How did you come by them?" Her eyes strayed to the bare patch on his left shoulder, the place he should have been wearing his badge. If he was a knight, good for us, because they got codes. If he weren't . . . well, I don't need to spell it out for you.

He leaned down, and he did look directly at us for a second.

"How do you think?"

He swung his leg off his horse and slid to the ground. He stretched in a way that suggested he'd been riding for hours. My mother did not take her eyes off him. He lifted his arms high in the air and bent his back. He smelled of the road and of danger. His sword hilts knocked together, and I saw him do that little motion that I was to see him do so many times, a hitch and a push at the hilt of his falchion to keep his swords clear of each other. He looked at us for a long time.

"How about I find you a fresh axle for that wagon?" he said eventually.

"That would be kind, thank you," Mom said. A touch of hope entered her voice. The knight had made no move against us.

He looked at the wagon. "You'll need to turn this in to the postmaster in Charleston."

"I cannot pay you if you ride with us," she said. She was lying; she could pay, but she'd have been a fool to tell him about the bride price hidden under the mailbags. My mother was no fool.

"We'll figure something out."

"I will not pay you in that manner." Her grip on my hand became fierce.

Quinn gave a half shrug that made his mail jingle. "I don't mean anything of that nature." He went to the pony and pulled out an oilcloth bundle and unrolled it on the ground. There were a number of tools inside, all in pockets sewn perfectly to fit them. Worn wooden handles and iron heads poked out of each. They looked like bald orphans tucked up in rows of beds in an orphanage, hopeful to be picked. He pulled out a small saw and a hatchet.

"There'll be a reward for the recovery of this mail wagon. If you'll see your way to letting me keep the money, I'll get you as far as Charleston."

"What about afterwards?" I blurted.

"I don't know about further north. It's bad country past the city, and out of my way."

"Please, mister," I said.

Quinn gave me a smile, tight, but friendly. "Maybe we'll work something out. What happened to the mailman? Was he on his own? No gunner?"

My mother nodded. "His gunner left him a while back. He always said he preferred to travel alone, and wouldn't take another partner." She nodded backward off the road, to where his corpse lay stitched into sacking behind a bush. "Such a stupid accident. The pothole there broke our axle. He fell. One moment he was talking, and the next . . ." she trailed off. Her eyes had gone a little pink. "He was a good man. A kind man."

"That's bad luck," said Quinn.

"Yes." She had more than her share of bad luck, my

mother. God did love to test her.

"You took care of him?"

"Of course. He took a blow to the head, but I was not about to take chances with my son."

"Wise," he said. He had this way of lading a whole sentence worth of meaning onto one word. "Let's see about that axle."

He went away for a while. We heard him chopping a tree. I made to go watch but my mother pulled me back and shook her head.

Fifteen minutes later he returned dragging a sapling. He threw it down on the floor, and went to his tool roll for a curved draw knife and worked it at the sapling's twigs.

"This will do, till we get to Charleston. It won't take us any further than that."

"It's got a kink in it, mister," I said. My mother shushed me.

"That's why it won't take us any further." He hitched up his belt, adjusting his swords again. "It'll break soon enough too. It's not seasoned. And bad timber round here, none of it grows straight." He looked into the dense stands of young trees crowding into the road as he said this, telling them more than us. "I could do with a hand, ma'am," he said.

"There's no need for that."

"What do I call you then?" He looked up from under his eyebrows, amused, but maybe—and this is the oddest thing—shy.

"Mrs. Hollister," she said. Her first name was Sarah, although she didn't tell him that until later. I always intended to call my daughter Sarah, after my mom. But the Good Lord didn't see fit to bless me that way. "This is Abney."

He nodded at me. I stared back.

"Then help me, Mrs. Hollister, and we'll be on our way."

They had to take the mail out of the back to lighten the wagon. I tried my best to help, but the sacks were bulky even if they weren't heavy, and most of them were heavy. Not once did Quinn look like he'd break the wire seals. Neither the king's law or the Dreaming Cities take kindly to mail pilfering, but I figured he could do just what he liked. Who'd stop a man armed like that taking what he wanted? He didn't so much as squeeze the bags to see what might be in them.

My mom was strong and capable. They worked hard, not a word between them, as they levered up the wagon with a pole cut from another tree. Quinn propped up the wagon base on logs and a couple of rocks. Then he fit the new axle, quick and clean. We took away the prop, and loaded up the mail again. That was that.

Last in was Walter. A good man, well liked in our village. He didn't have to take us. But he did. If his death had ought to do with us, I can't say. Maybe you think I'm some kind of draw for bad luck, like a few of the elders say still from time to time. You think that, think on this—without us, who would have been there to make sure he didn't go the way of the dead? He slept easy, Walter. That's more than some of us will get.

~

I was tired and Mom said I should ride in the back. I was ready for sleep, but I couldn't take my eyes from Walter. Mom had sewn him up tight, the proper way, one stitch through the nose to make sure he wasn't still with us. Stains spread from his head where the rock had done him, another from the back of the neck where my mom had severed his spine. Bump bump, the wagon went, sending old Walter rocking to and fro. What if Mom had missed? What if it didn't work on him? I couldn't stop watching, sure as sure that at any moment he'd make the moan of the returning dead, start thrashing about, trying to get out of the bag and tear at me. It was hot and stuffy in the wagon, fall heat that sets you up for a chill when night's in. The light shining through the canvas turned blue and dingy, and I tried to go to sleep. But every time

I shut my eyes, I thought of Walter coming back and creeping up to gnaw on me and my eyes flew open. Walter's corpse was a horrible shape in the dark. The canvas flapped on the wagon hoops, mailbags rolling, and Walter going bump, bump, bump.

I caught a few words up front. The wagon stopped. Walter rolled in his sack one last time. I swallowed. My throat was dry and my skin clammy.

Quinn rode up round the back. I didn't see him coming, being a mite occupied, so I near died myself when he lifted the flap.

"Not healthy, son, staring on the dead like that," he said. "Get out and ride up front with your mother."

I scrambled out fast as if ghouls had got a scent of me and were baying for my blood. My mom gave me a little squeeze. I was shaking something, and I needed it. It's a hard time of life for a boy, being halfway a man. Damn fool I felt like, staring wide-eyed like a kid the whole time at the knight. I shoved my mother's arm off, my cheeks burning, even though I wanted her to hold me close more than anything.

Quinn trotted up level to the driver's side, that big white horse of his glowing in the twilight.

"Thank you, sir, for looking out for my boy," my mother said. "You never told us your name." She hadn't said much to the knight. She was still wary, but he hadn't tried anything. Maybe she'd not asked his name to forestall any unpleasantness. Ask some men their name, and they think you're asking for a whole lot more.

"Quinn," he said.

"That's all?"

He nodded, looking down the road. "It'll serve," he said.

"And you are a knight?" she asked this cautiously. I could tell she was weighing up in her mind the need to know, against the need to not provoke him.

He gave his quick, crook-mouthed smile. There and gone. "For my sins," he said.

"But you wear no badge? Which city is your lord?"

"My choice, ma'am," he said, answering the first question but not the second. "We best stop for the night," he said.

"Here?" said my mother. The forest was thick still, the sky that utter black blazing with stars that you find yourself under out in the wild.

"Can you suggest anywhere better?" he asked.

We stopped.

He got off his horse. Conversation over.

~

Quinn tended to his horses. He had a way with them that

was kind and careful, and I lost some of my suspicion of him.

He caught me watching.

"You gonna help, son?"

I didn't move.

He shrugged. "This here's Parsifal," he said, slapping his horse's neck. "The little one is Clemente. Clem, if you prefer. He don't mind."

"Strange names," I blurted.

"The angels named Parsifal, son, they like to allude to old stories. They think it's fitting, funny. Clem though, I named him myself."

The pony shook out his mane at the mention of his name. Quinn strapped on his nosebag. They had an understanding between them, those three.

Several hours later, I twitched awake. I was lying on my back, the lumps of the ground pressing into my back. Half asleep like that, for a moment I thought I was lying on bones, all the bones of the dead past reaching up hungrily through the ground to devour the present. That woke me up for real.

The moon had gone. It was damn cold, not yet frosty, but that was only a few weeks away. I think the chill was what woke me.

Mom and Quinn were talking, the low, sibilant rumblings of adults being quiet. The voices they use when they're engaged in love, or arguing. Rarely any other time else.

Mom and Quinn were close to argument.

He and my mom talked hard, her trying not to shout, all hisses and bitten words, him slow and reasonable, voice mumbling like water. If they'd have known I was awake they would've shut up, so I kept still and listened, me being endlessly fascinated by the dealings of adults.

Adults think kids don't understand. My mom thought I didn't. She loved me, my mom, she would do anything for me. That's why she sold herself on to Gern after I turned eight. Keep me fed, keep me strong. I understood that, she never spoke with me about it, but I knew what she did. She didn't want to remarry, and even though Gern was good in his way, he'd still demand his rights. That must have been hard on her. I don't think she ever loved anyone after my father died. Same with all that travel to get me here. You might think about leaving this place, going somewhere else, but leaving's harder than just picking up your pack and walking down the road. There's the angels for one, they're not always happy with folks with itchy feet. Sometimes they are, sometimes they ain't. You can't ever tell. Then there's finding somewhere. You want to make it in the city, fine, but you want a new village? Good luck to you. They won't let you in unless you got something to give. My mom, she had something—she was fertile, but she wanted better than to just sell herself again. All her life she'd struggled to keep a bit of freedom and had never quite managed. But she didn't go halfway across Virginia for her. You might think otherwise, but I know she did it for me.

This is what Quinn and my mom were saying.

"I'll take you to Charleston. Make a new life for yourself there. I can't take you to Winfort."

"And what is there for me in Charleston, Mr. Quinn? How long until a man stakes a claim on me, and paid my bride price to the magistrate? Then what? If I go to my cousin, then he will vouch for me, take me in, and I will be free of marriage difficulties."

"You don't want another husband? Taking a man will ease your way some."

"Maybe. In time. But the choice will be mine."

"The boy needs a father." I could feel his eyes on me. I lay dead still. "This is a rough world, ma'am. Rougher still if you're on your own. You'll be the first to get thrown out if there's a bad harvest, or the dead come, or there's disease. You get your pick. You're pretty, still young, fertile too, and that's a rarity."

"If you are suggesting that my boy's interests are not my highest priority, Mr. Quinn, you are incorrect. I have to be careful. I don't want some dirt poor farmer working him to death, or him apprenticed in a filthy trade."

Quinn sighed. I heard him poke the fire, it burning harder after he did. "My point is, ma'am, why go all that way? Set the price high, that's your prerogative, and drop it for the right man. The road north of Charleston is dangerous."

My mother's voice hardened, an ugliness crept into it. She was stubborn, so stubborn it might have poisoned her if she'd lived longer. "All it takes, Mr. Quinn, is for some man to bribe the justice to judge my price too high and lower it by legal fiat. Then what? The power I have over my own body is tenuous at best. I need a man to shelter me so that I might freely choose. Under the vouchsafe of my cousin, we'll both be free." She was angry about this, she always was angry when she spoke on this subject. "Men with money are rarely kind."

"You chasing kindness might just get you killed."

"I'd rather chance the angels' wrath than have my boy watch his mother die miserable, and then him die miserable because of it."

Quinn grunted in agreement. They were silent a space. "It wasn't always like this," he said. "It won't be like this forever."

"It does not matter how it was," my mother said, "and I do not share your optimism, Mr. Quinn. God has reduced us to the level we deserve."

"Maybe," he said. "Why did you leave, Mrs. Hollister?"

"After New Karlsville fell, there was nothing left there. It is as simple as that."

"Things rarely are simple, ma'am. Let me see your letters."

Clothes rustled. She kept Cousin Matthew's letters close by her chest.

Quinn breathed out. I imagine he was reading.

"This the last?"

"Yes."

"And you got this five years ago?"

"Yes. His letters became less frequent, on account of the increasing depredations of the Emperor's Punishment, but he was still alive then, and he says life away from the river was good, 'cause the Emperor's Punishment didn't go that far north."

"Things change. The angels are unpredictable, their creatures more so." This from a man who was one himself. "The Lord of Winfort holds his lands at the angels' command, but that don't make him immune to the dragon. How old will your cousin be now?"

"Forty-one, he's eight years my senior, but we were very close when we were young."

"How close?"

"Friend close, Mr. Quinn! He was like my brother," she said.

"Alright, alright. Closer than that, things get tangled."

He was weighing up the journey. The danger. What was in it for him? Knights have honor and nobility and all the things they should have, but these great virtues weren't intended by the angels to be wasted on little folk. They are the levers and fulcrums of kingdoms. And no matter how well disposed to you a knight might be, they ain't hell-bent on suicide.

"You will be paid," she prompted.

"You're offering a lot of money," he said.

Mom must've told him about her silver. That scared me.

"It is."

I tensed.

"I'll try harder then to be accommodating," he said without rancor. "Alright. I'll do it," he said. "But from now on, you and the boy do what I say, when, and how. Your lives will depend on it. Are we clear?"

"I understand, Mr. Quinn." My mother's voice was light with relief. "Now that our business is concluded, I will retire. Wake me when it is my turn to take watch. And . . . Thank you, Mr. Quinn."

Quinn said nothing, but I imagined him nodding, and staring into the fire lost in thought. My mother bedded down next to me, letting in a draft of cold air as she lifted our blanket. Under her pillow of rolled clothes she'd have a knife in her hand. What she thought she could do to a man in full armor with a knife like hers, I don't know. But she'd have died finding out if she had to. A wolf howled out in the woods, and I shivered, wishing the fire were higher. My mother snuggled into me, bringing me her body heat.

"Hush," she said. "Hush."

It was a while before I could sleep again. My ears strained for sounds. More than that, I wondered how much of her money Mom had promised the knight, and if he'd kill us and take it all.

Fact of the matter is, it turned out she'd promised him half. We got a good deal, because the Emperor's Punishment, the dragon, roamed the woods between Winfort and Charleston, and our road went right through its territory.

~

My mother woke me in the morning with a gentle shake and a gentler kiss. "Get up, Abney, it's time to go," she said softly, breathing the words onto my face along with her love. For a second I felt safer than I had in a long time.

Gray cloud clotted the sky, thicker toward the east and the mountains I'd never seen. I smelled rain. It wasn't properly light, but dawn was close.

"Sun'll be up soon, we best be going," said Quinn. He threw a bit of wood onto the embers of the fire; bright flame leapt up out of the white ashes. "Son, your mom and me made a deal. I'm taking you all the way to Winfort. Make us some breakfast, and make it quick. I want us over the Winfield bridge within five days. The way should be easy going until we get there. Once we get over, that's when things will get hard."

"Do as Mr. Quinn says, Abney."

"Yes, Mom," I said. As if I wouldn't.

The Emperor's Railroad

AFTER TWO DAYS we came upon the Emperor of Virginia's railroad.

We heard the railroad before we saw it; the creak of wood and leather, iron wheels grinding on iron rails, the shouts of men, the clop of horses' hooves. Quinn took us a sharp left, down a long, gentle slope onto one of the great roads of the Gone Before. Roads are like rivers, they always join together to make a bigger road, then a bigger road, until you get onto one so wide you don't see what they was half the time, until you suddenly notice that this wide flat was made by *people*. There must have been a whole lot of people back in the Gone Before, to move all that soil and rock.

It was on the remains of one of these highways that the emperor had built his railroad.

The old road had been cleared right back to the bottom of the embankment. The amount of trees they'd felled was staggering, and the road again cut a broad scar through the forest that had hidden it for hundreds of years. With the full scope of the road revealed, it made me think what marvels they made in that age, before the angels came.

This hadn't all been done to awe folks like me. In the middle the emperor had made two new roads of graded stone either side of a rail line. There was a train going on by, forty horses dragging a line of three flatbed trucks piled high with lumber. Twenty men went with it, some to manage the horses and the flatbeds, the rest to stop either being stolen. Most of them were armed with crossbows and armored in mail, and prowled up and down the walking boards of the flatbeds.

The rails gleamed in the sun, stretching out in a long, lazy curve. The road on the far side of the railroad was reserved as a towpath for the rail horses. The nearside was free for the traffic of citizens such as ourselves.

Our wagon settled onto the paved road, and I was amazed at how smooth the ride was. After the emperor fell, the road hadn't been so well kept up, but compared to what I was used to it was like gliding over ice, even with the potholes and such, and that knotty bit of wood for a rear axle.

The rail horses plodded, the flatbeds moved slow. Our wagon was faster, and we outpaced them soon enough. I was glad, because I didn't like the way the guards were looking at my mom.

Civilization cut harder into the woods the closer we

got to Charleston. At first there were stockaded homesteads isolated in the trees. Brave people living that far out of Charleston, or those who like to keep to their own. The two go hand in hand sometimes. Maybe when you don't like other people much, the forest doesn't seem so bad. I sometimes get the notion that living in a town ain't what God intended for us, all rammed up close cheek by jowl, nosing into each other's affairs, all that sinfulness. The Garden of Eden sure weren't like that. Towns is God's punishment.

More traffic came onto the road. We passed another lumber train. Charcoal ovens and wood cookers stood in clearings. The number of farms grew, until the forest lost so much ground there was more farmland than trees, and stepped fields marched up low, naked hills. The walls round the farms got lower, became stout fences.

A view opened up, wider than any I'd seen before. In the distance I saw a city, the biggest place I ever saw. I stood on the seat to get a better look.

Quinn looked at me, the gawking farm boy. He nodded ahead.

"That there is Charleston," he said. "Second city of the Kingdom of Virginia."

"I never thought I'd see the railroad, now I'm seeing Charleston," I said. I think standing up high on the wagon and looking down on Quinn helped me keep my wits.

"This is just a spur, son. We're coming up to the main line soon."

Not long after, the railroad split in two and curved off to the left and to the right to join up with a double line. This was differently made, and I knew it instantly as work of the Gone Before. Sure enough the rails and all must have been new, but the ballast and the carved terrain it ran through were the handiwork of the ancients.

The road went over a bridge over the railroad, and merged with another road, this one also built on centuries-old groundworks, and very busy. On the far side of that was a broad river; the Kanawha, green and sluggish as a snake in winter.

The road crossed the Kanawha on a huge bridge. This was another of the works of the Gone Before, much patched and fortified, the first and last piers crowned by twinned stone gatehouses. We went up onto it. The gates were open, but every person was required to stop and pay a toll, and the traffic ground to a halt high over the water.

Another wagon drew up by ours. "You'll be here a while, kid! You'll have plenty of time to enjoy the view," said its driver. He was dirty, but honest dirty. His wagon bed was crammed with barrels. "I got a cargo of good cider here. Whenever I'm coming into town I'm thinking I'll be here long enough for it to turn. But you know what?" he said with a conspiratorial smile. "I always says to the old lady, well then, I'll sell them vinegar!" he laughed at his own joke. Quinn gave him a dark look.

"Mom?" I said.

The bridge was crammed with people. More people than I've ever seen. Fifty or so wagons, all types, wanting to get through, more coming from behind. People on foot, carrying baskets full of goods. All kinds of folks, all kinds of wares. Such a thing to be going to the city, and we weren't even in it yet.

"Alright, Abney, but to the side of the bridge, no further, don't go where I can't see you, and make sure you keep pace with the wagon when we get moving, it might appear like we'll be here a while, but you get lost in your daydreaming and we'll be through without you."

"Yes, ma'am," I said. Then I was off the side of that wagon fast, I had to see!

I went to the edge of the bridge. Walls of crumbling concrete bounded it. A cold breeze came off the water, but it was refreshing, and I laughed into it. It brought tears from my eyes. Fall is my most beloved time of year, that feeling you get from the mixing of all kinds of weather. You can feel the sun hot on your skin, hot enough to burn you should you take your hat off. But the air is often cold, and the wind colder still. It's four seasons all of a time.

Beneath me was a goods yard for the trains, a docks

beside. The main line of the Emperor's Railroad comes up on the south bank of the river. Trains take goods off the river, back overland to Huntingdon on the Ohio where they can be loaded up on boats again. The Kanawha joins the Ohio, but it was thoroughly blocked before the confluence, and there was the dragon up that way besides.

There were three big cargo ferries coming and going dragging themselves over on ropes, sail barges coming down the river from the east, but none coming upstream from the north.

On the other side was Charleston. The town's there on a spur of land caught between the Kanawha and the Elk. The rivers give good protection from the dead, but there's a wall fronting the river just the same on account of Virginia's frequent warring with Ohio. Broken blocks quarried from the buildings of the Gone Before made up its footings, stone on top of that, taller than anything I'd ever seen. It fair took my breath away, but Charleston was a mean old town. Five thousand souls cut off from the wild lands of the north by no more than ten feet of rock. It was more a fort than a home. South of the river is softer lands, Charleston's where Charleston is more for reasons of history than sense.

There was another, smaller bridge on the other side of the Kanawha, going over the river Elk into the city. Another gatehouse had been built across that. There were the remains of several other bridges on both rivers. They'd all fallen in, leaving their piers behind as vertical islands and their decks in the water as ragged weirs where they'd not been cleared. Charleston looked bigger than it actually was. An arm of the wall came out from the main part, running a few hundred yards along the river to shelter the northern docks. I found out that behind that wall, on the landward side, was nothing but ruins and pumpkin patches.

Outside the precincts of the present town were the foundations of the Gone Before. Around the town as much as could be had been torn down, the past scraped away to give an eyeline to the perils of the present. But even on the northern hills there were fortified farms overlooking the city, their terraced fields full of dead maize stalks and apple trees, and a couple of little villages too, thready smoke rising from their forges and fireplaces.

If I could have climbed those hills right then, I'd have seen nothing but forest on the far side. There were no men there, excepting Winfort. To the northeast it was even wilder. The further you went away from Charleston toward the southeast, the more evidence of people and their works you can see on both sides of the river. The Kingdom of Virginia's a patch of godliness either side of the mountains, but Charleston's a frontier city. To the west is Ohio. North is deadly country, a kingdom of monsters whose lords are the angels. Somewhere far north was the Dreaming City of Pittsburgh. But there wasn't any way through to get to it.

And we were heading into the very edge of the wildlands to the Winfort. It's still wild north of here, but back then it was wilder.

Nine tall chimneys came up out of the city, all of them pumping out smoke. There were more, if the columns of steam were to be trusted, lower than the walls. A harsh smell blew on the wind when it turned to the north; tanneries, chemical works, wood cookers. In the river were three dozen or so paddle-wheel platforms, moored to the bridge by thick chain rising up to the deck. These turned night and day in the flow of the river, making electricity. Charleston is a free town, they got a charter there and so some leeway for the science of the Gone Before. There are lights that burn all night. The angels don't mind it there. It is permitted. They were mighty proud of their lights in Charleston, kept pointing them out to me. Quinn thought they mattered not a horse's shit.

There were seven towers set into the circuit of the city walls. All were big, blocky, stone and scavenged concrete halfway up their height, timber the rest. All except one, bigger than most, made of new concrete and so being all smooth and of a piece. Stories back home had it that the Emperor of Virginia had the knack for making such, and that he had built that tower with old knowledge for his wars, and that was why they called it the Emperor's Tower. But that was before I was born, and stories is all I had.

Stories filled my sight that day. The works of the Gone Before were everywhere around the city and the river: concrete and moved earth, the greened mounds of ruins. Far out in the woods, the leaning skeletons of tall towers, and one topped with a dome like a cracked eggshell. They must have been such buildings, but these were a ways from the new town.

Truth is, all that's left of the world before is just hints for those who know what to see. If the river was a snake, then the old world was its sloughed skin, discarded and dead on either bank. The wooden houses and farms of to-day's people looked mean and small by the wreck of the past.

I took my hat off, let the purity of that wind draw out my joy, and a little sorrow besides. I'd not had time to mourn for my friends and kin in New Karlsville, I was trying so hard to be brave for my mom, and I did not want to trouble her with my tears. You got to re-member most everyone I knew was dead, dragged down by the unliving. All my friends, my teachers—hell, even my enemies, such petty and terrible ones as a youth can have. Confronted with all the ruin around Charleston, the corpse of the past alive with the work of men like maggots, something broke in my heart, and the tears coming out of my eyes suddenly weren't all down to the wind.

"Quite the view, ain't she?"

A man came up on me unawares. I blinked my tears away hurriedly, wiping them away on the back of my hand. I felt such a fool, snotting and blubbing like a baby. "Yeah, uh, yeah. I guess so."

"Say, my boy, are you alright? You appear to be a trifle discommoded, if you don't mind me speaking so baldly."

I shook my head, but I minded. Boy my age then doesn't like it when his weaknesses are there for all to see. The shame a boy that age can feel is mighty powerful.

"What's your name, boy?"

"Abney," I said.

The man made a funny expression. Of course that's his name, he seemed to be saying, why are you telling me? Everyone knows Abney!

"Pleased to meet you, young man. The name's Theo Germaine, an introduction that is as germane as the name." He chortled, then skipped over my lack of comprehension, waving it away with his hand. His other went to my shoulder and squeezed me companionably. He was a funny looking fella, with a dirty red jacket with feathers of all kinds hung along the seam of the sleeves like buckskin tassels. He wore a wide-brimmed hat with a kind of bowl-shaped crown I'd never seen before. His hatband had beads all around it, and more feathers, wrapped and dressed the Indian way, lying flat along the left side. A pair of goggles with smoked glass were about his neck, on top of a shirt as dirty as his jacket. He smelled of woodsmoke, liquor, and engine grease.

"What brings you to the fine city of Charleston, jewel of the Kanawha!" He said this in a way that could have been ironical or not. Like he was leaving it up to me to decide what he really meant, to see if I'd laugh. Men like that are dangerous, I had a sense of that even then.

"Passing through," I said.

"And where might a fine young man like you be headed?"

I didn't care for the way he was examining me. I tried to pull back, but he gripped my coat hard, wrinkling up my shirt and vest underneath.

"Just passing through," I repeated.

"A smart boy! Very wise to keep your doings close to heart." He released me and cupped his chin, patting his cheek with his fingers. "How's about I show you around? I know a good hotel, a better bar, and the best whorehouse. Good rates all, but I can get you a finer deal. My name's known about these parts, and the ladies'll part their legs for a fine-looking boy like you for less. You'll secure yourself a fine discount. What do you say, lad?"

I blushed a raging red at this talk of sex. He was hoping I'd hop along with him, a happy little frog right until the moment I jumped into the pot. I shook my head.

"No thank you, sir," I mumbled.

"Sir, is it? Sir?" The man's good humor was turning, becoming hard as a cobble. "I told you, boy, the name's Theo, Theo Germaine! Call me Theo, go on."

"Theo," I said.

"There, that wasn't so hard! Come, have a drink with me."

"I gotta be getting on, sir."

I made to step around him, get between a pair of horses and the wagon in front of them, but he blocked the way. I looked to the driver for help. He made no move, but kept on watching.

"Reconsider; you won't get a better offer."

I tried to shove past, but Theo was stronger than me.

"Let me by!" I said.

There was something sharp at my ribs. Germaine looked me in the eye, said nothing, as he panted his strong liquor breath in my face.

"Leave the boy be."

Quinn stepped out from behind the wagon. The driver stared at him too.

"What are you so interested in, friend?" asked Quinn.

The driver decided his interest was best directed elsewhere.

"You," said Quinn to Germaine. "This boy is with me. Are you detaining him?"

"Why, sir, I am only seeking to . . ." blustered Germaine. He held up one hand, drawing attention with it while he hid his dagger away. Quinn wasn't drawn by the ruse, eyeballing the knife, then staring at the man hard.

"Go seek somewhere else," said Quinn. "He isn't interested. You stick around, you might find that I am."

Germaine backed off, slipping through the traffic backward.

Quinn watched him go, then put a hand on my shoulder. "Be careful in a place like this, son, listen to the patter of a man like that, you'll find yourself on a Mississippi slave ship heading for the Gulf."

"I weren't falling for his uncle act," I said.

Quinn looked all around the crowd, alive to danger. Theo had wormed his way fifty yards down the bridge, and was talking to three men even dirtier looking than him. He glanced back at me. All the warmth was gone from him. He broke eye contact, and then he was directing his ruffians elsewhere into the crowd.

"Don't matter none if you were or you weren't. Men like that aren't above getting rough if the soft soap don't work. Be careful."

Charleston

WE PASSED THROUGH THE toll gates before noon. The guards there didn't ask no questions and gave us a chit for the Elk River gate once we'd paid up. Quinn had his horses hitched to the tailgate of the wagon and rode up front with me and Mom. She paid from the hoarded coins of her bride price.

Traffic moved slowly between the two gates of the Kanawha bridge, us touching down on dry land opposite the city walls for maybe ten minutes before we were off and over the second bridge.

It was by now early afternoon, and warm. The smell of the place was intense. So many people all together, the reek of the machines and works inside the city. Towers of white steam and black smoke poured upward. There was a banging and clamor from inside the walls so loud I thought I was about to pass into hell, and my heart beat to match.

From the Elk we got a better view of the city. The walls went sheer into the water, forty yards tall at least. But it was the Emperor's Tower held my eyes, so much grander than the patchwork masonry of the others. That tower was the most impressive thing I ever saw. It was all fresh made, not a bit of it picked off the carcass of another civilization, but something *we* built. That gave me a little hope for the future. There was another, tall tower, a little lower and a lot thinner than the Emperor's Tower. This was capped by a roofed belfry housing a massive bronze bell, and permanently manned. I recognized this alarm bell for what it was. We'd had one ourselves, back in New Karlsville. That so large and fortified a city needed one brought on a shiver of disquiet.

Hard men with wary eyes patrolled the wall, walking with the deliberate, slow-stepping swagger of soldiery. They were armed with muskets. I'd not seen so many guns in one place. I glanced at Quinn's six-shooter. His was a far more potent weapon, made with old knowledge from the Gone Before. That reassured me, somehow.

Quinn leaned in to me as we drew up to the gates. "Stay close. Charleston's not big, but you don't know it. There's more than one Theo Germaine in a place like this."

Fronting the Elk was a gatehouse, bigger than those on the bridges, its arch enclosing a massive pair of gates. They were tall, made of heavy wood faced top to bottom with steel plates. The gates and the portcullis behind were open, it being daytime, but heavily guarded.

The wagon in front of us went into the town, and a soldier liveried in blue and a dirty yellow that might have been gold if you squinted hard waved us forward. He wore a steel helmet with a sloping neck piece, and carried a slender sword and a heavy flintlock pistol. He was outclassed in every way by Quinn, but he was pompous enough not to notice.

"State your business in the city of Charleston," he said.

"Salvaged mail wagon, coming up from the south," said Quinn.

"You aren't the mail driver," said the guard.

"Salvaged, like I said."

"Where is he?"

"Dead. In the back. I came across the wagon and these two on the way here. I'm seeing them safe. They were traveling with the mailman."

"How did it happen?" said the soldier. He was looking over the wagon suspiciously.

My mother spoke up. "The wagon broke its axle. Mr. Quinn here replaced it for us. The driver fell, bashed his head in on a rock. It was an accident."

The guard wasn't entirely convinced. There's a problem with putting a reward on mail that gets lost—sometimes folks can get a little preemptive, trying to scoop up rewards for solving misfortunes they made themselves. It's a stupid thing to do, mail robbers get hung no matter which city or kingdom you're in, but it don't stop people trying. The guard looked at Quinn's armor, his swords, his gun and his snowy white horse tied to the back of the mail wagon. Outside the walls it was very still. The noise of the town was louder than ever, the people, horses, smith's hammers, clatter of workshops. There were a crowd of people at our backs, all yammering away, but it felt quiet. The rivers cast a spell on the place.

"You are a knight," said the guard.

"Yes," said Quinn.

"I thought your kind were all dead."

"Most. Not all."

"We haven't seen any knights in Charleston for a long time." The guard looked for Quinn's badge on his shoulder. "You've no heraldry. Which city are you sanctioned by?"

"Doesn't matter," said Quinn.

The guard's eyes narrowed. "It's my business to ask your business, knight or not. Who is your mortal lord? To which of the angels' cities do you owe your fealty?"

"That doesn't matter either."

Quinn and the guard stared each other down a moment. My mother was getting anxious. Quinn radiated unfriendliness.

"You sure you're a knight?"

"I'd be dead if I weren't," said Quinn. "Dreaming Cities don't take kindly to imposters."

"Depends how long you've been imposing," said the guard. "You might last a week or two."

"I might, but I've been a knight a sight longer than that," said Quinn.

"The two you found. Where are they headed?"

"That's their business."

"Where are you headed?"

"That's mine."

"You are not helping your case, sir," said the guard.

"I'm a knight, servant of the angels. I don't have to say what I'm doing. Most times, it's better if I don't. For all concerned."

This exasperated the guard. "I need something. I have my own duties. Writing down what your business is in our city is one of them."

"North," Quinn said. "I'm taking them to Winfort. They have kin there. We're here to rest and resupply."

Now the guard snorted. "You're suicidal if you want to head to Winfort. Nothing but bandits and the living dead, that's if the dragon doesn't get you. The Angels of Pittsburgh don't want anyone heading that way."

"That's the way we're going."

The guard stepped aside. "That's your choice. Good luck to you. Go to the post office, off Clendenin Street.

You'll have to make a report. If your story checks out, you'll get your reward."

Quinn nodded. "It'll check out."

The guard waved us on. He was already losing interest, scrutinizing the next would-be entrant.

Mom geed up the horses, and we went into Charleston.

~

Through a cool tunnel of vaulted stone, and out the gates the other side. A burst of sunlight and noise welcomed us. There were people everywhere. Shops and stalls lined both sides of the roads. So much color, so many voices all talking at once. All kinds of people, some of them as weird looking as Quinn. There were workshops there at the base of the tall chimneys, the stink of Charleston's industry. Hammers ringing on forges, arguments, music, so much noise! The main street kept to the boundaries of the Gone Before, and was wide. The shattered concrete of it was patched with square-cut stone, and more recently, concrete again.

"Post office is this way," said Quinn. He steered the horse off up an intersection. This road narrowed sharply, the margins of it built over with the constructions of our own era. The main road I could handle, it being broad and open to the sky. But there timber buildings crowded in, chunks and scraps of ancient structures incorporated into their fabric. Crowded though it was, the street preserved the uncanny straightness of the towns of the Gone Before, and we came out onto another wide road. On the far side was a squat stone building, solid as a fort, roof topped with wooden turrets in the Virginian style.

We crossed the street, and went into the post yard through a double gate. A couple of mail workers in uniforms took the horses' bridles and looked at Quinn with grave suspicion. The older of the two said something, and the second ran off. The first hitched up his belt, and stood his ground.

"I've brought this wagon in. Found it on the road," Quinn said.

The mail worker patted the horse's neck. "This is Lincoln. He went out with old Walter."

"That's right."

"Where's Walter at?"

The other post worker had come back with a couple of friends. All of them had drawn swords, short slashing blades. One carried a stubby shotgun.

"In the back."

The older mailman's nod sent two of them round the tailgate of the wagon.

"He's dead," said Quinn before they got there.

"He's right, sir."

"Get him out," said the mailman. "Is this your doing?"

"No."

The mailman pursed his lips doubtfully.

"I am a knight, not a bandit," said Quinn.

"And where is your proof? You have no badge."

"I have my seal." Quinn reached for the fastenings of his mail vest.

"No! No, leave it. I won't be thanked for bringing the attention of the angels down on us."

"Suit yourself," said Quinn, and let his hand drop. "I'll be needing to speak with your postmaster."

"Yes, you will." The man didn't look pleased. "I'm Hanneger. Come with me."

Quinn followed the man out of the yard through a side door. I slipped down off the wagon seat and followed. My mom called my name, but no one made to stop me.

The backways of the post office were narrow, and crammed with sacks and boxes. There were several doors opening on rooms full of people sorting the mail into racks. Electric lights buzzed feebly over them; the windows were real narrow, good for guns, not sunlight. There were a lot of men clutching paper, moving between the rooms in that purposeful way that men with important jobs have, forcing me to dodge or be knocked down. The first four ignored me, but the fifth barred my path and clapped his hands on me.

"And where do you think you are going?"

"Mr. Quinn! Mr. Quinn!" I shouted.

Quinn had reached the far end of the corridor. He turned back.

"He's with me," he said.

If the mailman was surprised to find a knight in his domain, he did not show it. "He shouldn't be back here. This is royal territory. He could be hanged for this."

"I said, he's with me," said Quinn. He took my arm hard and pulled me past the man.

"Got quite the talent for trouble, haven't you, kid?"

"Sorry, sir."

He let go. "No harm. You stay close by me. And don't say a word, you got that?"

I nodded mutely. Hanneger was waiting impatiently at a door down the end.

"Postmaster Friend is within. You sort this out with him, or you won't be leaving this place."

"If you say," said Quinn.

"Well then." Hanneger opened the door, and ushered us in.

Postmaster Friend's office was well proportioned. With four of them gun-loop windows in the wall it had a fair amount of sunlight. He had electric light too, but this was weak and supplemented by a handsome spirit lamp on the desk that whooshed pleasantly. Friend was a fat-faced man with spectacles. He had a visor on his head, to shade his eyes from what, I ain't got a clue to this day. It was dingy in that office. His clothes were fine, his belly round, and his hands soft. To me he looked ridiculous, but then I hadn't ever seen a rich man before.

His attitude was a world away from Hanneger's.

"A knight!" he said with a bright, wide smile. "I hear we owe you a debt of gratitude."

"I'd settle for the reward," said Quinn. "Man's got to eat."

There wasn't a hint of animosity from this little fat man. He laughed and clapped his hands, delighted by Quinn. "Of course! We'll see you straight. Please, come in, sit down. Can I offer you a whisky?"

Quinn nodded for the drink, but did not sit down. I did.

I'd never sat in a chair like it, padded all round, and on some kind of swivel. When I discovered that, I swung myself back and forward until Quinn clapped his hand on the back to stop me.

"It is very fine to see one of your sort here again," said the postmaster, handing over his glass. "We haven't seen a knight for years."

Quinn knocked back his whisky in one and hissed

through his teeth. "Not that many of us left," he said.

"Yes, yes," said the postmaster. "A lot of war and trouble these last decades."

"That's about it," said Quinn.

"I would have thought your numbers would be replenished."

"Since Columbus fell, there have been no more knights made, by the will of the angels."

"The Lord does move in mysterious ways," said the little postmaster. He refilled Quinn's glass.

"Don't he just."

"Well," said the postmaster. "A knight! The city will be abuzz for weeks. Can you perhaps relate to me your purpose here in Charleston?"

I thought Quinn would not say no, but I was surprised.

"I'm on my way west, as it happens. Plan to skirt Columbus. Business of the angels. I've agreed to take this boy and his mother on to Winfort before I do."

This surprised the postmaster. "Columbus? There's nothing but plains of glass there, sir! Fair took the wrath of the Lord on itself in the war, that city of the fallen angels! Gone the way of the Gone Before and all the other wickedness of the world, and that is no bad thing. We remember it only as a byword for evil." His eyes widened, face open as the pothole that had killed Walter, begging for an explanation to fill it. "And Winfort first? The curse of the angels still lies on the land between here and there, worse further north. This whole region is yet to recover from the war. What with the wrath of the Lord coming in hard on Columbus, and the dragon keeping Ohio and Virginia from tangling afresh in the marches, I don't know if it ever will."

Quinn ignored the man's concerns. He ignored his fishing for an explanation harder. "I'll not be stopping long. What are the roads like to Winfort?"

"You know the area, sir?"

"Some. I've not been out this way since the war."

The postmaster scratched under his visor. He had bad news written across his face.

"Not a whole load of trade coming this way from out of Ohio. The princes prefer to deal with the north, up the Ohio under the watch of Pittsburgh. We're losing trade. Lord Corn at Winfort's the only one in the wild. People are just heading straight on out to Huntingdon. Between you and me, it's getting worse every year. This town ain't what it was. We've had no contact with the Winfort. Ohio ain't that keen on us. Columbus destroyed by Pittsburgh at the Lord's command, Jackson burned off the world by the emperor's armies, they've not forgiven Virginia yet. It's a sorry state, sir, that's all I can say. I hope I never see another war with men and angels on both sides. It's always we little folk that lose out. This boy and his mother are lucky to have a knight to hold their hands, yes, sir. These are challenging times."

"What about the railroad?"

"Oh that's fine right the way through to Huntingdon. Get you there in a day or so, then you can get yourself a riverboat up the Ohio."

"I mean the way north, the spur over through Winfield on to Point Pleasant."

"Well, we used to get a lot of folks coming down that way." He frowned. "Only, it ain't seen any traffic for five years or more. The dragon's all riled up. It started swimming the river and coming into the Bend about, oh, about twenty years back now. There's no one there now at all, those as weren't burned out left of their own accord. We shut the tollbooth some time back, and the bridge hasn't seen much work on it for eighteen years or more, none since the dragon began its marauding. It's hard to believe that when I was a boy not much older than you"—the postmaster spared me a smile at this point—"there was talk of resettling the Bend, blasting through the Winfield rapids to open the way direct to the Ohio, but it came to nothing. If you're intent on braving the dragon, then you go careful on that bridge. Wood's getting rotten so I hear. We'd patch it up ourselves but . . ." He shrugged and smiled, an adult gesture that I couldn't decipher, but which I suspected meant they just didn't care. "I figure once you get out into Pleasant Valley you'll be right as rain, yes, sir. But that was in the old days, and rumor has it the dragon has started to intrude on Lord Corn's lands." He frowned. "No, no on second thoughts, I really can't recommend it." The man swallowed, and blinked again. His eyes were froggy behind his glasses. He thought he was being foolish and presumptuous, but he was brave enough and kind enough to warn us anyway.

"Winfort's still there?" asked Quinn.

"Yes, yes, I believe so. The dragon lets that be, for the time being at least. But the land around it? None can say. Communications between here and there are cut, have been for, oh, getting on for seven years. I won't risk my mail wagons that way. Might I suggest another way? I wouldn't cross the Kanawha, sir. Get a boat out of Huntingdon like I said, take you all the way to New Virtue. There are post roads in Ohio, good and straight. The boy and his mother can get a boat north, and come down on Winfort from above."

"That'd be worse," said Quinn. "No man wants to go into the forests up that away."

"I know it's out of the way, sir, and risky like you say. But there is no dragon that direction. Only the dead." He gave a short, apologetic laugh. "If 'only' is an apposite term."

Quinn huffed; the New Virtue route was a hundred miles out of the way. More.

The postmaster's voice dropped. "The dragon kills most folk who try to go through its territory."

"Anyone seen it?"

"One boy. Hunter. Stumbled onto the railroad tracks of the main line, raving and half dead. He said he saw it, well into Pleasant Bend. It's getting closer ever year."

"Where is this hunter now?"

The postmaster bared his teeth, an odd expression. I'd have said aggression but he was too good-natured. Postmasters have to be diplomats. I decided the conversation was shaking him. He had yellow teeth, crooked and poorly spaced. He nipped the tip of his upper lip between them. "He died not long after coming into town. That was four months gone. Nobody has been that way since, and nobody wants to try."

"I'm not interested in Huntingdon. I'm headed north. Tell me about Winfield. Say I get a boat like you say, can I get there if I come in from Point Pleasant?"

"Well, that town's gone! Burned out twelve years back. You see, sir, I meant it sincerely when I said about the dragon. The people are dead or fled. It's getting so dangerous we reckon that it won't be long until the dragon turns its attention on the shipping going up and down the Ohio." He smiled sadly, inviting Quinn to join him, to share the misfortune. Quinn did not smile. The man blinked, taken aback.

"There's no ferry at Point Pleasant anymore?"

"No, sir! And no bridge neither. The emperor's bridge there got burned up not long after the dragon came. And you won't get a riverboat captain worth his salt stopping in that vicinity at all. No, sir, they're all afraid of the dragon, they power on through like the wrath of God is on them, which it would be, sir, if they were to stop. No expense in charcoal or coal spared. You want to go to Winfort, you go via the river and head further north, come down through the forests. That's my advice."

Quinn was displeased by this news.

"We're worried here it won't be long before the Emperor's Punishment comes upon us. We got men watching the northeast every day, but we worry it ain't enough. What can we do? We can't move the city. We can only pray that the dragon moves on, or the angels take it away. Time was we blessed the name of the emperor, but we won't speak it now, no sir. A curse on him, that's what we all say, for what he brought down on us all here."

"The emperor did a lot for this country."

"The emperor," said the postmaster, stiffening. "His pride. We all suffer for it still, praise the Lord for his mercy in punishing us gently for our sins." The man dropped his head. He looked up at that moment Quinn was supposed to say "amen," but did not.

"Will that be all, sir?"

"How about that reward."

"Yes, yes, of course." The postmaster poured himself another drink. He drank it with unsteady hands. This talk of the dragon had shaken him up.

Quinn looked at me. I looked at him. The dead terrify me, but I wasn't scared of a dragon. No danger of losing your immortal soul if you die by one of them.

The postmaster went to a tube set into the wall, and shouted into it. "Are the seals still on the bags?"

A tinny voice replied. "Yes, Mr. Friend. Still sealed, and all the right dates and codes."

Friend smiled apologetically at us. "Some of the bandits have become inventive, stealing the mail and resealing the bags with copied cramps. All of them have got their own codes stamped into the leads now. I am sorry if it appears if I doubt you. It's all standard procedure."

"No concern of mine," said Quinn. "It's a good procedure."

"It helps," said the postmaster, a little mollified. "Anyway, as I am sure you heard . . ." He went to a small iron safe and unlocked it with a tiny key, all alone on a ring at the end of a chain. He withdrew a double-skinned cotton bag and passed it to Quinn.

Quinn hefted it, reached into his pocket, and tossed Friend a big silver dollar. Not one from his reward purse, but one from a kingdom I don't know. It was an odd shape.

"I shouldn't really," Friend said, in a way that suggested he really wanted to.

"Not for the reward. For your being accommodating and giving us the information you have. Keep it."

The man clutched the coin to his chest and bowed his head, a little salute. Rich men stay rich taking whatever money comes their way. He paused, wanting to say more, not sure if he should.

"Thank you. Do be careful, sir. There aren't enough of your kind left."

"Maybe. There are stories growing around the knights, and they aren't all true," said Quinn. "I ain't no hero, but we'll be careful." He put his hand on my shoulder, and steered me out of the postmaster's office.

We left by the front, and back in through the big doors to the post yard. The mail wagon was being unloaded; the horse had gone. Quinn took his own animals back, checking their packs quickly. The mailmen paid us no attention, and we left.

We spent the next few hours buying supplies with my mother's money. Every street corner showed me another marvel, and I was dragged away from them all. Quinn did not want to stay within the city walls longer than he needed to, and by late afternoon we were out of Charleston and heading north.

The Road to Winfort

WE KEPT TO THE HILLS on the west side of the Kanawha, avoiding the old towns to the north of Charleston.

It's best to steer clear of the towns of the Gone Before. If you don't got business going in there, then don't. But in the valley there wasn't much left to avoid. Charleston had once stretched well up the river, occupying all the flat lands on the banks. Not that you'd not know it. The modern town looked huge to me, but in truth it had become tiny.

Sometime after the Fall the Kanawha had heaved itself out of its bed, moving in when the people had moved out. Some of the old streets were a maze of pools that you'd only know for being streets once by their shape, and that was the kind of place bad things wait for you to happen by. Bandits—they're the worst to my mind, the living preying on the living. And if there weren't many dead men lingering in the valley, there were enough.

Me and Mom and Quinn passed from Charlotte and followed the railroad west toward Huntingdon and the docks there on the Ohio, but before long we turned north, following the emperor's overgrown northern line for two or three miles. We left the railroad and went up into the low hills to the west, wary of what we might meet on the flatlands, even that close to the city.

On the ridgeline we felt safe. The valley had been full of buildings, now it was thick with woods. Real dense, the sort of thickets that'd trouble a wild pig. On the opposite side of the river to us were many of the dead places, sunk in the river or swallowed by the forest. Dunbar, St. Albans, Jefferson. These are places that are no longer places, names for stretches of woodland only a learned man can tease out from old books. I only know their names because that's what I did.

The ridges were clearer than the flat. The road of the Gone Before that ran on the west side of the river had been cleared by the emperor's armies for his railroad and his war. But after the emperor had overreached himself and fallen foul of the angels of Pittsburgh it'd been abandoned again. I can't tell you how that railroad brought it home to me, how puny the works of man are compared to those of the Lord. Thirty years old that railroad was. The main east-west run was fine and shining, but the north was a wreck. Sleepers rotted in their bed. The rails of the first five miles had been picked off and taken away. Trees and bushes erupted through the road and towpath.

The emperor clearing the old roadway for the railroad made the woods down by the river even worse to travel than they were before. His men had piled up everything they'd no use for alongside. There's all manner of junk hidden under the poison ivy for long stretches, making it a really good place to get ambushed.

Where we had to go through the villages of the Gone Before we crossed them quietly and as quick as we could, us on Quinn's big white horse, him alongside jogging silently but for the jingle of his armor. Most of these places were nothing but grouped platforms of concrete hidden in the woods, or lonely shaped stones poking through turf and litter. I was hoping to see some of the carriages of the Gone Before, the marvelous carts without horses they rode, once upon a time. When I was a kid I was told they was all the colors you can think of, gold and blue and red, all as glittery as a beetle's wings and smoother than polished gold. But there weren't none. I asked Quinn where they were and he said they'd gone to rust long, long ago. He showed me some black crumbly stuff one night that he pulled out of the soil.

"They thought their world would last forever. This is all that is left of the things they thought eternal," he said. "This was plastic, stuff made in the Gone Before. You won't see much of it around no more. It's a fine lesson in hubris."

"Amen," said my mother.

I was real disappointed.

Sometimes the horses' hooves crunched on broken glass hidden by the vegetation. But if there'd been houses there, they too had rotted to nothing. Mostly we knew we were in a place of the Gone Before when Quinn pointed out a lot of mounds that told tales on the remains hiding underneath. There was one fine sight, a fat-bellied tower half in the water, taller than the hills around it. Looked like an unfinished clay chimney pot, still on the potter's wheel. Solid enough to last the ages, covered in a web of green crawling plants like a vertical forest. It amazed me, then chilled me.

From up high in the hills traces of the old world were easier to see—a patchwork of squares in the woods; areas where the trees are tall, ones where the trees are short. It's funny. In places where there are men, the Gone Before might never have been, them little signs of what was scoured away by what is. But in that place, where people had never widely settled again, you could see a time of wonders picked out in shades of timber. It makes you understand why some folks think the Gone Before were giants. I came to the opinion that we're best off away from all that out here, where there never was much and still ain't. It makes a man feel peculiar to see it all laid low, those works, makes you look at your lifetime's effort and see it as nothing. We have the promise of heaven, sure enough, but folks like to make their mark on the world. You look at the likes of that tower and you start wondering what the point is.

Take my advice, don't ever go into the old places. The ghosts there call tears that can't be stopped, and you're not ever sure why you're crying them.

We had to come down off the hills to get to the bridge. We skirted a rank old lake full of reeds. The edges of it were lined with stone or concrete, and you could see it had been much bigger once. Now there was a pathetic puddle of open water in the middle, home to a few ducks. From there we went into a place that had been the southern part of a place called Winfield, and now was a boggy wood.

There was one building standing, all made of stone. The mortar between the blocks was delicate as sand, looked like one gust would blow it down, but it stood.

Quinn didn't so much as look at the building as we went on to rejoin the railroad, him being used to such things and all, but it sure took my attention. Beneath the choking vines I saw a flash of something bright. We were all going on foot then, so I walked over to get a look.

There was a big window in there behind the leaves, glass so pretty and smooth even under the dirt and grime. It was all colored to look like a picture. Stained glass like what we have in the church, but much bigger, and cleaner cast, no imperfections in it. Old work. You could just make out the picture under the dirt. I saw a cross, a cross of Christ the Lord, radiating out the rays of God's love. Like us, them before had their churches.

Quinn joined me. "Church of God." He pointed out a bunch of letters to the right of the window, hidden by creepers. They were carved into the stone but real soft edged, almost rubbed out by time.

"Ain't no other kind, mister," I'd said. After that business with Germaine, I was trying to show him how much of a man I was—twelve years old, and not scared by no knight with his two swords and his gun! Of course I was scared. He shrugged at what I said.

"Is it the same?" I said. "Did the Gone Before follow Jesus?"

"Some," he said. "Maybe not enough."

"Is that why God struck them down?" I asked.

Quinn didn't answer me. Instead, he said, "It's a miracle that glass is still in there. That's a rare sight."

I was uneasy. I could see the clouds through the clearer bits of the window, like someone had put it there as a message, just for me. "Is that why he sent the angels, because they were ungodly?"

Quinn led his big white horse away.

I saw something else there in the leaves. Gray bones,

very old. A skull in the angle between the church wall and the ground. I've seen plenty of dead, and them dead that come back, but that skull there on its own affected me more than any. It couldn't possibly have been there since the Fall, but I thought it had. I made a little noise. Quinn's horse flicked its ears at me.

"Be quiet now, kid," he said. He patted my back absentmindedly, the same way he adjusted his swords. Something he did without thinking. A little further on there were signs of more recent dead about, their stinking scat and the gnawed bones of a wild pig. So we went quick and quiet through the wood that had once been a town. We saw none of the returned, not until we got to the foot of the bridge where that pack surprised us and Quinn had to kill them again.

I had nightmares about that church for years, that window in a forest clearing all on its own, all other traces of men gone from its vicinity. In my dream I'd call out to God but he didn't hear. There'd be nothing but animals and the dead men, eating and pissing around the wall and its glass cross still gleaming a thousand years old, a mound of skulls piled on the ground before it as an offering.

～

So, that's how we got to the Winfield bridge, most of the way to Winfort. From there, our troubles were about to begin.

By the time we had set up camp on the bridge, it was getting dark. After a week together my mom and Quinn had fallen into an easy routine. He'd set the fire, she'd find spots for the bedrolls and go about fixing dinner. First we all scavenged about the bridge, gathering sticks from the feet of trees growing out the concrete. He stacked them close to hand, in the spot where the smoke was most like to go, wet wood closest in to the heat. That all took time. When he figured we had enough, Quinn pulled a bundle of kindling sticks off of his pony, built a teepee out of it, lit it with a big-headed match, and coaxed a little fire into life.

A thread of blue smoke rose upwards. There was no wind at all. Past the churn of the weirs made by the broken bridge and the dam further down, the river was as smooth as glass.

"We need more wood. Come on, son," Quinn said, beckoning at me.

We worked quickly gathering sticks. Night was coming in fast. You could hear the smallest sound, loudest seemed the crack of the fire as the wood took. The sky was getting so dark and deep that I stopped and stared up at it. After near two weeks of traveling I still couldn't get used to the stars. We kept the lamps burning all night long in New Karlsville, just like we do here, it kills the depth of the night and makes the monsters seem further away. The sky was a deep purple, so full of lights, the wide band of the Milky Way cutting across it.

"It's something to see," said Quinn.

"Up on this bridge, floating in the sky, I feel like I could fall into them."

"Now that is not a comfortable notion," said Quinn.

"No, sir."

"Time was, you couldn't see them. The world Gone Before was too full of light, lights in the houses, in the highways. Like in Charleston, but more of them, and brighter."

"How'd you know, mister?" I said.

"I know, is all. I read. I've been places, and I've heard things. Once you get as old as me, you'll understand."

I shivered. I wanted the tiny tongues of flame to hurry up, eat the wood and make me warm. Quinn jerked his head back toward the fire. He dropped his pile of wood by its side, took my sticks and put them atop his, then went to Clemente. He yanked a blanket from a pack and threw it at me. It was musty, smelled of leather, saddle soap, and horse. My mother wrapped it around my shoulders with a worried nod at Quinn.

Something crashed through the brush on the far

shore. I started at it. My mom shushed me. Neither she nor Quinn spoke.

We ate of the food we'd got in Charleston. It occurred to me then that although Quinn was well equipped, he was poorly supplied. He wolfed down his meal like he didn't know when he'd next eat. There never is enough, even for a knight, no matter how many fields you plant or crops you sow. You might get a couple of good years until the damn dead rise up, tear it down. It's worse when you're on the road. Hard tack and jerky, a cup of beef broth made from paste. Go hunting in the wrong place, sin enough to bring the angels down on you, scare up the dead, come across someone meaner and more desperate than you are . . . And no matter how mean and desperate you think you are, there's always someone who is meaner and more desperate. It's a wonder there's anybody alive at all.

An hour after the moon came up my mother made me turn in. She sat up a while, opposite the fire. Quinn stared into the flames, his thumb pressed into his lips like he was silencing himself. My behind was cold, but the fire was warm on my face and chest and I was tired. I tried not to fall asleep, thinking my mom and Quinn might talk again. But they didn't say a word and soon enough I'd gone.

New Karlsville

THAT NIGHT I DREAMED about New Karlsville. I still do, from time to time. I wish I didn't.

If there'd been a Karlsville before New Karlsville, I do not know. There might have been, and a Karlsville before the Karlsville before. Meeting Quinn made me want to learn whatever I could. I read a lot, most anything people can find me. One thing I learned is that a lot of the towns, a lot of the cities, they got names from people who lived in these lands before the Gone Before even came here. Names from the Indians that used to live all in this country, or names from countries far out on the other side of the ocean, places that give us our way of speaking, places that no one from these parts has been to for a long time.

When the anniversary of my father's death came around every year, I got sad. Still do, as a matter of fact. My stepfather Gern had words to say about that. He used to say that people never die. Not in the meaning of the churchmen and our eternal place at the Lord's side. He meant right here on Earth. Gern said the dead leave a part of themselves in things like names. He said that if we failed God's second chance and that the dead were to rise up tomorrow in so great a number so as to wipe every last one of us from the Earth finally and forever, then after every last farm and town was torn down there'd be lumps and bumps in the forest to remember us by, telling the story that we were, even if there's no one left to see it. Maybe, just maybe, God will make something new that might do better in his creation, this next thinking creature will come along and dig up what we left, and wonder at who we were. I don't know what I believe about that, as I said, I wonder how long those traces will remain afore they're all gone.

So I had no idea if New Karlsville was the first or the second or the fifteenth place of the name. It was the last, that's for sure, and it was my home.

In purpose and size Karlsville wasn't much difference from Winfort. Somewhere to live, small—three hundred souls maybe, mostly farming. We kept to ourselves. I was born there in the year of the Dominion of the Angels 1097. My father died when I was six, taken by a poison fever after he trod on a copperhead out in the fields. Mom married Gern when I was eight, and although he was always good to me, I never saw him as a father.

We had schooling, a church, smiths, store, wood ovens, mill, all the rest. Two hundred and fifty acres under the plow, a little more for pasture. The country was less wild than here, even now with the King's Peace on the land. It was a kind, gentle place, right until the end, when it wasn't.

I was woken at night by the alarm bell clanging. Men were rushing to the walls, bows and long pikes in their hands. We drilled for this over and over.

There was pounding on the door. "Abney, Abney Hollister!"

Mom came into the front room where I slept by the fire. She was scared looking. There was a lot of shouting outside.

"Get your clothes on, Kaley Josson is here for you."

"Abney! Come on! You're needed on the walls!" shouted Josson from outside.

We didn't let the women fight in Karlsville, like most places down our way. The women were too valuable, they're the only ones who can make new life, after all.

The front door banged open. Josson, a rangy man in his late thirties, pushed into my room. There was a gaggle of other boys with him. He was our youth marshal, leader of us boys. "Get a move on, Abney! The bell is going, the bell!"

I struggled into my pants and boots. I hadn't time to do my laces, and was still hooking my suspenders over my shoulders when I ran out after them. Josson was riled up, scared mostly, I think. I don't blame him. He shoved my leathers at me.

"Get these on!"

I shucked them on. They were too big for me still. Willy Keevors tied up the back for me. We stopped for a second so he could do that while I knotted my laces. That got us another holler from Josson.

The bells were all ringing, on the wall, in the church, and in the schoolhouse. Bells everywhere. Men were up on the platform round the walls. The walls were split wood planks, reinforced and cross braced, but just wood, not the stone as we have here. The first of the oil flasks went off, tossed off the wall by a hothead. A tall cloud of fire burst up, spitting down on over the outside. In the gaps between the planks I could see flickers of movement. The swaying shamble of the returned dead.

Josson shouted us up the ladders. Willy went up before me, and he stopped dead at the top.

Willy looked back down at me, his eyes wide with horror.

"There'n thousands of 'em!" he said.

"Get your ass up there, Willy Keevors!" bellowed Josson, and Willy stumbled onto the wall walk.

All us men and boys wore thick hide coveralls. The style we had down our way was like an apron with arms. You stepped into it, did it up at the back. The front had a long bib that covered the front down to your boots, but was open over the legs at the back so you could move. Thick gloves protected our hands. We boys didn't get the masks the men wore; close-fitting leather that covered their heads, faces, and necks. First time I saw my father dressed up in his dead fighting gear, I screamed the house down.

Pity is, that's one of the few memories I have of him.

Karlsville didn't have no metal armor like the men here, cowhide is thick enough to stop the teeth of the dead, for a while, anyway. There was no war as deep into Virginia as we were.

Boys helped, they didn't fight. We pushed on past the men over to our station, a platform coming off the main walk stacked high with clay pots. We were the firemen, you see. The turpentine and pitch bombs the men used to burn out the dead sometimes caught the walls. It was our job to douse the flames that got into the wood. Josson clambered up a viewing pole where he could look up and down. He had a white stick to point with. We were supposed to watch him all the time, but I was standing up on my tiptoes, trying to see out over the wall. I'd got a glimpse of the dead out there. New Karlsville was used to bands of the dead, ten, twenty strong, sometimes as many as fifty. But this time there were hundreds of them, maybe more—a great rising, all staring at the fort walls with them dead eyes of theirs. Now I couldn't see nothing but the laced-up backs of the men in their leathers, no matter how much I bounced on my feet to see.

A couple of the men stopped in front of us—Josson's brother, who was a lieutenant of our militia, and William Mason, who was a mason on nights other than such as that. Mason was taller than Josson. With their gear on, that and their voices was the only way of telling them apart.

"They're all around the walls."

"This thickly?" said Mason.

"And more to the north. Take one in three men off here, get up to Toscin's position, and reinforce him."

"There's not enough here as it is!"

"Keep your voice low, Mason!" Josson glanced at we boys, shivering there next to our pots of water.

Thunder rumbled. Unusual, I remember thinking. Thunderstorms are a day thing. You rarely get them after midnight down there, and this was two, three in the morning.

Mason went off at a jog, tapping men on the shoulder and pulling them away.

The line that was left after Mason took his reinforcements looked mighty thin. The men worked in threes, an archer next to a man with a pile of rocks—good sharp ones the size of three fists. The rockman had two or three turpentine bombs. The rockman and archer were protected by a man with a long pike, but often as not the pikemen were taken away in groups. Their role in that kind of situation was to push off the dead if they began to climb atop each other, or to stab them in the head if they were pressing too hard against the wall. On the ground a good wall of pikes is fine proof against the dead, but it's a thankless weapon. In a formation, you got to hold the damn thing over your head if you're in the third row. On the wall, you're hanging over the side. Fifteen feet long, that was our standard length in Karlsville, heavy with it.

Rain fizzed in the wall torches. A quick wind blew out flags of fire from each. The sky lighted up, and the pikemen looked up nervously. We had lightning poles on the wall every thirty feet, but they dipped their pike heads just the same.

Thunder boomed. The skies opened, and the rain pounded on us.

"We're not going to have much to do," I said to Willy.

"Yeah, yeah." His words were shaky. That boy was flat out petrified.

"They're coming! They're coming!" shouted someone.

The dead moaned, loud like, like a herd of cows lowing. Their feet squelched in the mud. A scrabbling came at the wall.

"Bombs, ready!" shouted the captain. He was a

farmer. The man next to him was the smith. Another guy the town weigh master. What a man was in the day did not matter. That night we were all warriors.

The rock casters lifted up their clay pots. These were fired nice and brittle. They swore something terrible as they tried to get their oil rags to light in the rain, dangling them into torches held by their comrades.

"Throw!"

All around the fort, guttering flames arced up through the air and fell down. They shattered on the ground and on the dead. A mix of turpentine and pitch burst outwards in sheets of fire. The dead moaned loudly at the pain. They hammered on the stockade. The gates creaked in their frame. The fires burned in the downpour, but they weren't as effective as they should be with all that rain.

"Archers, loose!" cried the lieutenants. Arrows whistled out from bows. The archers held five arrows in the hands gripping the bows, flicking them into position when each shaft was shot. This way they could send down a storm of arrows. They emptied their hands quickly, pulled up more from the quivers hanging off the wall, and did it again.

"Second bombs, throw!"

Another rain of fire whooshed out, tall mushrooms painting us all in orange and red. With that moaning and that fire, it was a scene right out of hell. I have no doubt what to expect if I'm judged wanting at the gates of heaven. Whatever Satan has in store can't be any worse than that night.

The third round of bombs went. Then the rockmen began casting out their stones. The thwack of arrow into flesh and the wet smack of rocks on bone jostled in my ears with the moans and the crack of thunder. Lightning speared down, some ways off.

"Boys!" Josson was pointing his stick some fifteen yards down the wall to the left.

"Come on, Willy," I said. He and I hefted up two heavy pots a piece and ran from the platform. The other boys waited on eventuality.

We ducked and weaved our way through men shooting and throwing and stabbing. Where we were going was obvious; orange light burned constant there.

"Here! Here, Willy, come on!" I shouted. A pikeman leaning over the edge fell with a scream, yanked over by the dead pulling on his weapon. He was alive when he fell into them, and conscious when they ate him. I can't shut those screams out, not ever.

There was a sheet of flame licking up the wall, a bomb had bounced into the stockade, most of the pitch had gone on the wood rather than the dead, and the lower quarter was afire. The dead scratched at the burning wall, pushing each other into the blaze, heedless of their flesh cooking as they did. There were more burning in the crowds, lighting up a sea of rain-wet heads and outstretched arms. Lightning flash picked them out in hard white. There was a big group round the gates, pushing rhythmically against them. Men leaned out over the parapet there, jabbing with pikes and tossing rock after rock into them, but it didn't do any good. More of the unliving were heading that way. They've an instinct for weakness, the dead, same as wolves picking on the sick and old.

Willy froze, mouth hanging at the number of them at the gate. I poured our water down the side. But even with the rain, it weren't enough to douse the fire.

"Willy! The fire, get the fire!" I tugged at his sleeve; he woke up enough to upend his pot down the wall. It spattered and hissed, but did a whole lot of nothing in putting it out.

"We need more water! Come on!"

We ran back to the platform, snatched up more pots. My arms were going to burn in the morning, I was thinking.

There was a deafening crack. I thought the storm was coming right overhead, but there was a splintering sound, and the moan of falling wood.

People started shouting all at once. It took me time to catch a clear indication of what was happening. "The gate! The gate's fallen!"

The dead were pouring through the gateway into the village. The men on top were working both sides of the walkway. The town reserve formed up in the middle of the square. The ground was kept clear for twenty yards inside the walls for just this eventuality. Their formation of pikes moved down the street, trying to push the dead back out of the gate, but there were so many our men were surrounded, and the dead ran in without hindrance, coming up the stairs to the walls, heading off into town. The church rang its bells faster, the signal to retreat.

"Boys! Get off the walls now, get to the church before it's locked up. Get to your mothers, there's not much you can do here," shouted Josson. He came down from his perch to join the others.

Willy and I ran. The dead were coming up onto the wallwalk the other way from us. My God, these ones were fast. They must have fed recently, and they were vicious. The men dropped their pikes and bows and drew machetes. Their hide armor gave the men some protection, but the first rows were knocked over by the ferocity of the dead's attack, and more than a few plummeted from the walkway into the mass of the unliving surging around the pike porcupine behind the gates.

In the square there were dead everywhere. Men were screaming, screams like that pikeman pulled off the wall had made. I'd taken my part in repelling attacks before, but nothing like this. I'd never heard screams like that, the sounds men make when they are torn apart by ragged nails and blunt teeth while they're still breathing. If it hadn't been for Willy, I might have frozen up and gotten myself killed, but he was more frightened than me; keeping him safe kept me thinking.

Lightning flared. Men were coming in from the north wall, shouting and running, hacking into the outside of the mob swarming round the pikemen. Maybe they should have waited, formed up and attacked at once, that's what good sense would suggest, but everyone was in a panic. The horde of the dead was still pushing through the gate, scattering into the village and putting the pressure on the pikemen badly. There were men there watching their brothers and sons pulled down and killed. There's only so far discipline goes in a situation of that gravity.

The pikes managed to keep the dead back for a while, but one or two of the dead ducked under, then three or four, and then ten or more, until there were too many to be cut down by the machete men tasked with dealing with those that came through. The pikemen of New Karlsville must've sent two hundred of them zombies to their second death, five for every living man, but the dead were near limitless. Once a formation like that collapses, it goes all at once. Order broke down, and the dead fell on them.

"Come on, Willy!" I shouted, gathering my wits. Both of us had been staring at this carnage for a good few moments. "We got to get to the church!"

That was enough to get his legs moving. We ran on, dodging stragglers from the horde. There were figures up on the north wall. Lightning showed me that they weren't no living men.

The church was ahead, a couple of oldsters and women beckoning at us. Three other kids fair flew through the door ahead of us. They were going to shut the doors.

Half a dozen dead or so came at a shambling run from behind the town smokery. They were on us. We only had ten yards to go.

The rain was merciless, soaking us all, making that leather so heavy and wet. We were slowed by it something awful. You ever have those dreams where something bad's coming and you can't run away, like your legs are made of gelatin? That was what it was like for real. Maybe that's what made Willy stumble.

He fell, and they leapt on him.

The worst thing you could do in those leather aprons was roll over and show your unprotected legs, and that's what Willy did. They aren't stupid, the dead, and they were on those legs so fast, teeth biting hard through Willy's pants and Willy's skin. He was screaming my name, holding his hand up for me, screaming "Abney! Abney!" over and over.

I wish I could say I went to help him, but I couldn't. I looked at the doors. One more boy made it before me, then the elders on either side looked one another in the eye.

I couldn't move. A moan made me turn. There was a dead man coming for me. My mind screamed at me to run, but my legs weren't listening. The stench of him made my head swim. I can still see him reaching for me, them terrible teeth clacking.

Then my mom was there, burying a knife in the head of that dead man up to the hilt. She grabbed my arm, yanked me backward with uncommon strength, and I fell through the church doors.

The elders swung the doors shut.

There was pounding on the other side, then the most god-awful screaming that went on and on. Then nothing but the booming of thunder and the moans of the dead.

The church had no windows. The walls were made of dressed logs and earth. It was our fortress of the Lord. There was no way the dead were getting in there. There was me, my mom, and a hundred and twenty or so villagers. The very old, the very young, and most of the women. There was no room in that place. There were two that got bit and needed a merciful end, and the smell of their blood filled every corner of the church. It was hot, and after a few days it stank. We came mighty close to running out of water, but then the dead moved on.

We came out to find our homes destroyed and most of our men dead.

There weren't enough of us left to make a go of New Karlsville, though some stayed to try. A couple of dozen of us headed out to other places, seeking their fortune in bigger towns or with their kin. That's what my mom decided to do, taking us north here to Cousin Matthew.

"They got stone walls, and armed men to keep the armies of the dead away, and the dragon in the woods keeps the armies of the living away too," she said. "The lord there was granted the land by the angels themselves, for his services against the traitor-emperor. We'll be safe there." Truth be told, I don't really know why we left. Sometimes a person gets desperate enough, or is scared enough, to grasp at any straw. After losing two husbands I don't think my mom could stand to stay in New Karlsville any longer.

A few days later old Walter passed us on the road. He'd been through the village, seen what happened. He offered us a ride to Charleston. But you saw what happened to him.

Willy's screams haunt me to this day. If you think that I was brave in that battle, but scared and jumpy afterward in this story, you'd be right. Now you know why.

~

I came up out of my dreams screaming, arms flailing, trying to push a dead man away that wasn't there. My mom had her arms around me, but I was so scared I was slapping at her face.

"Shhh, shhh! Abney! It's Mom, shh, it's your mother."

She was always there for me, my mom. She came out of that church and buried a knife in the head of that man trying to eat me. She was there for me again. She held me a long time. Me, who only a few weeks gone thought himself well past the need of his mother's comforting.

After a long while, my mom got me to lie back down and I quit my bawling. She was asleep quick. I couldn't. Some time later, my eyes were drawn by a movement in the sky.

A group of the stars moved, swiftly coming in from the east, bright white. Not stars, I thought sleepily. Angels' Eyes, keeping watch over us all, just like Preacher Relnik used to say.

I felt better. I fell asleep again, knowing that God could see me.

A Knight of Atlantis

MORNING BROUGHT CLOUDS OF mosquitoes that bit and worried at us while we packed up. Not much was said; Mom and me were quiet and scared of what lay ahead, and Quinn didn't speak without being spoken to. The sun showed us hills over the river a couple of hundred feet high. I wanted to get up there, away from the river and the swamp on the plain. After coming off the bridge, the railroad followed the river, running on the north shore toward Point Pleasant. The emperor had wanted to open up the port there as a rival to Huntingdon. It didn't happen that way. Once the war was won, the angels of Pittsburgh turned on him for his sins, and Huntingdon kept its hold on all the trade. The whole north section of the line had fallen into ruin.

There'd been a small town at the far end of the bridge. The whole thing had been burned down to black stumps. Charcoal don't rot. If it weren't for the fireweed growing thick in each building shell you'd think it all happened yesterday.

Winfield has a name that suggests a town back in the

Gone Before. You couldn't tell. Past the sorry remains of the recent town, swampy woodland came right to the water's edge, old trees overhanging the water as hoary and broad-girthed as if they'd been there forever.

The bridge that end was scaly black, scorched by fires hotter than I can imagine. The rails had a heat bloom on them where they weren't rusty.

"The dragon did this," said Mom. "The emperor made his war on Ohio with the angels' blessing, and built his railroad to do it. But then he turned from their light, so they cast him down and set the dragon on the land and forbade anyone from settling here."

There was a sort of breathy exultation to her, like she was carried away by the righteousness of it. Looking back on it now, I think my mom was looking for certainty in our lives, and you don't get much more certain than the judgment of the angels.

"It's more complicated than that," said Quinn.

"How do you mean, Mr. Quinn? The emperor overstepped his earthly authority, and he was punished for it. Amen to that."

"I mean there were two cities involved in that fight, Columbus versus Pittsburgh, angel versus angel. The emperor played a dangerous game getting between them. That's what I mean."

"The angels of Columbus were corrupted by the foulness of the Earth, the emperor started with noble intentions but was tainted by his war against them. What you say is blasphemy!"

Quinn clucked his tongue. "That it may be, but it's also the truth."

I looked at my mom. Walter had said that the army of the dead that killed my kin were part of the angels' wrath on Virginia. We'd had nothing to do with the war, and it was inconceivably long ago to a twelve-year-old boy, so that troubled me. I was brought up to believe in the infallibility of angels, that they came down to Earth to set mankind back on the path God intended. But I was getting older, and stories of the war didn't sit right with me. I didn't know what to believe.

And Mom, she was acting weird that day, jumpy and argumentative. We were all nervous. Even Quinn; there was a tension to him. He rode his horse, so we were walking by the pony. Quinn said he needed to be ready and that he'd stand a better chance mounted. He didn't say against what, but we knew he meant the dragon. He put all his armor on, and had assembled a long lance from sections he pulled out of a leather tube on Clemente. The things that poor beast had to bear.

There was no sound of life near the shore. The rumble of the river rushing over the mess of concrete from the Gone Before stopped being peaceful and became a menacing growl. Every time a fish flipped itself out of the water we jumped. Rumor held that the dragon was often seen near the water.

We went quiet as we could, Mom and me holding the pony's reins. More for our comfort than his need to be led, quick breathing as we jogged to the hills over the river plain. The swamp made us keep to the raised causeway of the Emperor's Railroad. Weeds and brush grew up out of the ballast between the sleepers. With no trees over our heads, we were exposed. It wasn't far from bank to hillside, but it seemed miles.

Quinn raised his hand. We stopped dead in our tracks. My mom's hand found mine. Quinn rode onto the railroad's edge, and I saw why we'd halted.

The way was blocked by a dead engine made all of metal. Its upper part was melted to bubbled slag, the cylinder to the front was bashed in and ripped wide open. The entire machine was scabbed a uniform red by rust. But even completely wrecked, the engine remained seated on the rails. All eight wheels sat immovably atop their metal path, defiant as an animal caught in its den.

"This is one reason why the dragon came," said Quinn quietly.

"A steam engine!" I said. I'd seen one or two. Several in Charleston. "I've never seen one with wheels."

Mom shushed me. She went pale looking on that

slaughtered machine. "It is against God," she said. "This is not a wholesome place."

"This kind pulls trains instead of horses," said Quinn. "The ones you see in the chartered towns are fixed. Those pump, make electricity, heat, drive workshops. But in the times before, they used them to pull trains."

"Why'd he make it?" I asked.

Quinn shrugged. "The war." He left it at that, didn't explain any more.

I imagined the dragon unleashed by the angels, all scales and fire and wings. In my mind's eye I saw it ripping into the engine, breaking it to pieces like that, melting the steel with its breath.

"If the angels sent the dragon to destroy this, and they overthrew their friend," I said, "why do they allow engines in places like Charleston?"

Quinn looked back over his shoulder at me. "Sometimes the angels change their minds, you'd be well to remember that."

A bird croaked off in the brush. The forest was unusually silent.

"We should be on our way. Dragons lair close to where they are set. They're made that way." Quinn kicked his horse on, passing by the wrecked engine on the slope of the railroad's bed. The brush was thick there, and it was tough getting past. I slipped on something, and I looked down to see my foot on a grayed bone. Noticing one, suddenly I saw lots of them, like they were leaping out of the earth all around the wreck. My eyes slid to the swamp, I knew what I was going to see there, skeletons half-visible in the murky water, plates of rusty armor all around them.

I fixed my eyes on Quinn's horse, and didn't look down again.

The railroad curved round to follow the Kanawha and we left it. The hillside rose up in front of us. Quinn clicked at his horse, urging it off the railbed and through a pool of black water. Parsifal surged through, snorting as he came up on the slope of the hill. Black muck caked him up to the haunches. Quinn turned him round and he waited as me and my mom crossed, dragging Clemente behind us. He didn't like that water. Mosquitoes bit at us relentlessly, the day was thick and damp and we were sweating miserably.

The hills beckoned. There was no road there, we were cutting directly through the woods. It was hot, hard walking. All the while we were straining for sounds of the dragon, but there wasn't any sign of it.

There's a certain irony in life, all our days is shot right through with it. Turns out we were worrying about the dragon, when we should have been worrying about the dead.

~

At the top of the hill the air lost its humidity. A fresh wind dried our sweat. I was ripped by thorns and stung by plants. I itched from a dozen mosquito bites, but I was still alive, and for that I was thankful.

"We'll stop here for a little while, get our breath."

"Is that wise, Mr. Quinn?" said my mom.

"No sign of the dragon," he said. "If it was coming, then it'd be here by now. We need to eat. Drink some water. We need our strength up, we don't want to linger here."

We sat on a rock. There was a break in the trees that afforded us a view back down the river. In the distance you could see the smokes of Charleston rising up into the sky. So much effort to travel such a short distance.

Quinn moved his swords so that he could sit, and fished a piece of jerky out of a pouch, then offered the bag to us. I was hungry, and stuffed some into my mouth.

"Chew it, Abney!" my mom scolded. She passed me a water flask.

"We crest this ridge, then down the other side. There's a valley on the north that leads down into a bigger one. We follow that. Winfort's ten miles north of here. If we're lucky, we'll be there by the time it gets dark," He took another piece of jerky and chewed it slowly.

"I do hope so, Mr. Quinn," said my mother. "I do not wish to expose Abney to another night camping rough, especially in an area such as this." She stood up. "Now if you excuse me, I must relieve myself."

She left the clearing. I wish I'd stopped her. I've wished that every single day since.

Quinn looked at me. "How are you bearing up?"

I shrugged. "I'm okay," I said.

"Your mom tells me you're brave. That you helped defend your town."

I shrugged again. I couldn't hold his eye. I didn't feel very brave. I hadn't ever since I'd watched Willy being torn to pieces in front of me.

"How old are you, boy?"

"Twelve." I felt about six, small and impotent.

"Well, that sounds brave to me."

"Why are you always so down on the angels?" I asked. "You are their servant. Don't they get mad at you?"

He swallowed his jerky. "Yeah, they get mad with me. But I don't lie about them. Some things are too serious to lie about. And I swore an oath to be truthful, as much as I can."

"An oath to the angels?"

He nodded.

"But you're still down on them. They are the right

hand of God upon the Earth. You're gonna burn in hell for what you say about them, mister. The angels know everything, and they speak your sins into the ear of the Lord."

"Your preacher tell you that?"

"Yes."

"You believe him?"

"Yes."

Quinn sighed and shifted his position on the rock. "Son, the angels aren't all they're said to be. When I was made a knight by them, I felt like you do. All the word of the Lord and the will of the Lord. I was proud. I was glad to be their instrument. But I found that their promises aren't good. I've been through a lot, all because of the angels." He paused. "I fought in the wars of the emperor. On the Virginia-Pittsburgh side. I saw things in that war no man should see."

"I've seen bad things."

"Yeah, well. You have. Truth is, when you see so much death and suffering, you begin to question why it's done, and in whose name. When I saw angels fighting angels, what the hell was I supposed to think?"

He was deadly serious.

"If they're both of God, why are they fighting? If both sides are good? The emperor asked these questions too. Pittsburgh used him to fight their war, and when they were done with him, they cast him down. They call it the emperor's war, truth is, the emperor's war was a war between the angels of Columbus and the angels of Pittsburgh. You hear what your momma says about the Columbus angels, that they were tainted by their time on Earth."

"Everyone knows that!"

Quinn inclined his head. "Maybe they do. But do you think the men who fought for Ohio believed their angels to be fallen, or did they think those of Pittsburgh were the ones turned to evil?"

I stayed silent.

"Same with the emperor. All of Virginia and more besides allied to the Pittsburgh angels, he was on the side of good, so far as the story gets told now."

"He was evil. He betrayed the angels after they helped him win."

"He was a man," said Quinn. "He was vainglorious and ambitious and wanted power, but I believe he wanted it to make the lot of people better. The more he learnt, the more he questioned. What we're told has it the wrong way about. He helped the Pittsburgh angels, and they supported him for it at first. Then he pushed too far. Things like that steam locomotive down in the valley. He went too far in using the old knowledge. So they killed him, set a plague of unliving loose on Virginia, and put the dragon here. Some say the dragon's here to keep the peace between the east and west. But the Emperor's Punishment is a weapon of terror, a thing meant to keep us scared."

Quinn was angry about this, there wasn't a flicker of it on his face, but his eyes, usually so cool, they were burning.

"But, why? Why did he do it?"

Quinn kicked his leg out in front of himself. "You go into any group of people, you'll see them complaining about this and that, how such a thing could be done another way. Every man ever born thinks he knows how to save the world, but most of them sit on their hands. The emperor tried to do something about it."

We sat a while, listened to the wind sighing in the trees, the surprisingly hard clatter of dead leaves falling to the forest floor.

"Did you meet the emperor?"

"Yeah, yeah I did. He was a man like any other, clearer sighted, maybe. Clever. Too clever." He looked me deep in the eye. "And I met angels too."

I had a sudden and fearful apprehension. I stood up and backed away.

"This is a test. You're not a knight."

Quinn watched me with his eyebrows raised, curious as to what I'd do next.

"I am a knight. And I did meet the angels."

"Then why don't you wear a badge?"

He looked at the floor. Another pause. "That's my choice. Way I see it, no matter what the angels intended for us knights or how they used us, I took oaths that I believed in, and I failed one of those oaths. The way I see it, I don't deserve to wear the badge of my mortal lord, not until I put things right."

"I don't believe you."

Without looking at me, he undid a clasp on his hauberk and pulled out a smooth rectangle of metal, about an eighth of an inch thick and big as Quinn's palm.

"This is my seal," he said. "I don't show it, because when I do the eyes of the Dreaming Cities are drawn to me. Here," he shrugged. "It don't matter none."

"I saw the lights in the sky."

"Did you, now? Well, you know they're watching already, see what I'm going to do, so it makes no difference if I show you this or not."

I couldn't tear my eyes away from the metal. Quinn was battered and filthy, but the seal was made of adamant, the angels' metal, and had no flaw. I thought for a moment it was a forgery, a clever mockery made of silver, then the sun caught it just so.

An image leapt from the seal, tiny but perfect and solid looking as you or I. A cowled angel with a bowed head standing over a city of spires set in a sapphire sea. Four miniature tall ships appeared. They were perfect in every detail, with flea-sized men clambering in their rigging. The sails snapped open and the ships sailed the air around the angel. The angel spread its wings out behind ships and city. I gaped at it, this perfect picture swimming on thin air. The mark of a knight, the mark of the angels.

Quinn spoke with a clear voice. "I am a knight of the Dreaming City of Atlantis, sanctioned by the angels there. This is their seal, and my authority."

The angel looked up, its face lost in blue shadow. Its hands rose slowly to the cowl, and made to pull it back. A sense of foreboding took me. I was afraid to see its face.

Quinn closed his fingers over the badge and the picture froze and faded away. I looked from the seal to his face and back again.

"An angel," I said. "A real angel."

"Son," he said. "The angels. They're not—"

He never got the chance to finish. A shrill scream cut the air.

"Mom!" I took off in the direction of the cry.

"Wait!" Quinn was after me, his mail jangling. His falchion rasped from its scabbard.

My mom wasn't far away, in a hollow bordered by young oaks. A lone dead man grappled with her. She had her arms crossed, braced against its neck to keep away the teeth snapping at her face. Its hands groped at her fore-arms, trying to tug them apart.

Her overdress was off, but her undergarments and petticoat were in place. It must've caught her just as she was finishing up.

The thing was wearing armor, not much different to Quinn's but so rusty as to be brown from head to foot. Incredibly, it still had a helmet on. Such details you notice at a time like that. How long had it been wandering around the woods, a dead man armored for a war two decades over? In places the leather was rotted through, and some of the plates hung off it, clacking dully as the zombie thrust itself against my mother. A foul smell came off it. Stepping into that hollow was to immerse yourself in its stench, it filled the space as surely as water.

The thing had sallow skin, blue-tinged around the lips, and those icy eyes common to all the dead.

"Mom!" I screamed.

Her head whipped round with dismay. The unliving growled at me.

"Abney, no! Get out of here!"

She was distracted by my appearance. There's no doubt in my mind that what happened is my fault. The dead man sank its rotten brown teeth into the blade of her upturned left hand. The soft flesh there parted like plum skin.

"Mom!" I screamed. She screamed louder.

Seeing my mom in danger like that robbed me of thought, and I flew at the unliving. Literally flew, I couldn't feel my feet touch the floor, I've never moved so fast.

Quinn was faster. He grabbed my shirt, yanked me back hard. I went down heavy, cracking my elbow on a rock. My arm exploded with pain, and I cried out.

Quinn barged at the dead man, sending him staggering. His rush knocked Mom down, but the dead man kept to his feet. Quinn shoved the zombie back with a kick to the stomach. Some distance gained, he swung his falchion viciously at the dead man's head. The blade bit deep into rusted steel, and it gave with a crunch, but the metal protected it and the dead man did not die again. It lunged for Quinn as he tried to pull his sword free, and the knight danced back, his weapon still lodged in the zombie's skull.

The dead man tottered in place, its head swinging back and forth between my mom on the ground and the knight. Quinn crouched, circled the dead man.

"Come here! You! Hey!" He clapped his hands together. This drew the monster's attention away from Mom. Quinn tackled it, mailed arm up in front of his unprotected face. This time the unliving toppled backward. Quinn scrambled up onto its chest, pinning its arms with his knees and holding the mouth shut with the heel of his hand. The thing had some power left to it, and it bucked under the knight. Quinn knocked his falchion clear of the dead man's skull with his forearm, snatched it up and sprang backwards. The zombie sat upright, bringing its head toward Quinn's next swing.

The falchion cut clean through the neck, rusted mail, moldy old leather and all. The zombie's head bounced to a standstill by the side of the hollow.

Black blood welled up from the neck stump and the body fell over. Quinn spat, then spat again. He was covered in rotting blood, and was not wearing his mask.

"Wait there!" he said. "Stay alert, that one's well fed, been living its death a long while from the look of its gear. There might be more of them."

He ran from the clearing, leaving me by my mom's side. She had her bitten hand cradled up against her chest. She was sobbing silently, keeping the pain in check. She was strong that way.

Quinn came back. He had a bottle of spirit and a leather case with him. He uncorked the bottle, swilled his mouth out with it, spitting the spirit away from him, then did it again. He quickly wiped down his sword with a rag, then again with a second soaked in the spirit.

He grabbed my mom, made her look up at him. "You know what I have to do," said Quinn.

My mom bit her lip. She unbent her wounded arm from her breast, and laid her hand out on a log. The other gripped mine tight. We both closed our eyes.

"I'm sorry, Mrs. Hollister," Quinn said.

His falchion blurred down. It made a cleaver's thwack as it hit my mom's arm.

She screamed. When I opened my eyes, she had her arm up again, blood pumping from it in such amounts I thought she'd die there and then. Quinn had his little case open displaying needles ready to close the artery and the skin. He tied off her wrist with a tourniquet, then set to work.

On the log her hand remained. The pale brown skin was robbed of life, the red meat at the end a sickening contrast to the moss it lay upon.

Quinn's Gun

QUINN WAS QUICK, and skilled. He stemmed the bleeding, but Mom lost a lot of blood. She was gray, moaning. Swooning from shock. Quinn picked her up, and hustled me along in front of himself.

"What's going to happen?" I said, though I full well knew the answer to that.

"If we can get her to Winfort, she might have a chance." He laid her down, and rearranged the packs on his pony. "You, get up here on Clemente. We're all going to have to ride. It's not far, so the horses should take it, but it's not going to be comfortable."

I scrambled up, trying to find somewhere on Clemente's back where I wasn't going to fall off. Quinn half helped, half hoisted Mom up onto Parsifal. He mounted up behind her, and wrapped an arm about her waist.

"Okay, son, I'm going to have to go at a fair lick. Hang on! If you fall off, get back on. Clemente will wait for you, and he'll find me again."

He spurred his horse into a run. The woods were

thick and the slopes uneven. We couldn't go at a full gallop, but Quinn and the horse wove their way in and out of those trees faster than could have been safe. Clemente followed with no guidance from me. It was all I could do to keep my head down as branches whipped past me, tearing at my clothes and my face.

Parsifal came down off the slope. We were into a shallow valley, heavily forested. Another low hill rose up on the far side. There was a little creek, and a flat shelf cut into the hill above it spoke of a road of the Gone Before. Parsifal went faster, leaving me and Clem a little behind for all that the stallion was carrying two people.

The valley went round a couple of turns, then Quinn drove Parsifal up the other slope, not so high this time. The horse bounded up with its back legs pumping. Quickly we were up and onto the summit, a hundred feet or so, then down the other side.

A wild roaring shook the forest. A tree cracked and fell down with a crash deep in the woods.

The dragon was awake.

Quinn's horse picked up speed.

We came down into a bigger valley. Thick woods, another flattened space that suggested another road from the Gone Before. They made so many roads. We followed this, and after a time we came out into an area cleared of forest and scattered with sun-bleached stumps. The bed of the road became a road for real, rutted and potholed but clear of vegetation. Parsifal broke into a gallop.

The cleared area became farmland. Farmsteads appeared, all walled with earthen banks topped with palisades and set far back from the wood's edges close in to the road. The road surface became smoother. Ditches lined either side. Quinn was far ahead of me with my mother, Clemente labored after, each breath a snort.

The valley widened. The cleared area crept up the hillsides, until the forest edge had been pushed back over the summits. Watchtowers, spindly, open things of wooden scaffold with a platform atop each, crowned three of the hills. Pumpkin patches, cornfields, cabbages, and pasture jostled them against one another on the valley floor, each one small and hard by its neighbor.

We were in the lands of Winfort, a tiny strip of habitation on the edge of the great northern Wildlands.

A flash of sun on white stone, and there was the castle itself, with a high keep and long sweeping walls of ashlar. A lower earth wall topped by wicker gabions followed the stone wall about one hundred feet out in front of it, and this was studded with large stakes angled at forty-five degrees. You couldn't see it from where we were, but there was a deep ditch between the earth wall and the stone.

Furious bellows chased us along the road, faint as distant thunder drawing nearer. We sped toward the castle.

People were working the fields. They looked at us with open hostility. A tongue of forest intruded near to the walls from a nearby hill. There was a large rock there, stained black, the ground around it bare. Chains dangled from its front. I did not like the look of that.

They call themselves kings, these men in their high castles who rule countries like Virginia. Men like the emperor, or our current King Jonas, but they can't control such wide lands themselves. That's why they need the lords, and why the lords are mostly left to their own business.

I had a mighty bad foreboding what manner of business this particular lord was about.

The passage to the fort was wide open. No man rode out to stop us, no shot was fired nor arrow loosed. The road was clear of traps, passing through the protective berm via a simple gap. There was no bridge, but an earth causeway lined with logs broke the ditch. This we also crossed, coming nigh to the walls.

Two men pushed the gates closed as we approached. A man leaned over the parapet.

"I am Jebediah Coppergather of the Winfort, castellan and gatekeeper of the fortress of Lord Corn. State your business!" he shouted.

"I am a knight of the Dreaming City of Atlantis! I request sanctuary here as is my right and the order of the angels," replied Quinn.

"Then where is the badge of your master?"

"I choose not to wear it."

"You have shamed yourself?"

"I have failed in a duty important to me. I do not display it as a mark of my shame."

"And the boy, and the woman?"

"They are under my protection. This woman, Mrs. Hollister, has kin here, a cousin."

Words were exchanged. My mom's head lolled on a weak neck.

"The name of this cousin?"

I spoke up, my voice sounded reedy compared to those of the men. "He's Matthew. Matthew Scout. Please let us in!"

More words. Precious minutes trickled by, carrying my mom's life on with them. The bandages on her wrist stump were wet with blood.

A man came to the parapet, peering down. He had prematurely white hair and wore the smock of a smith.

He looked at my mother, then said something inaudible to the armored man.

"Mr. Scout cannot see the woman's face," said Coppergather.

Quinn delicately lifted up my mom's head by her chin. She moaned.

"Could be her," I heard Matthew say.

"She got a letter from you, sir, a letter from you to her." I got off Clemente, and walked up to the wall. Crossbows took a bead on me.

The man, my cousin, looked down from that distancing height. I might have well been appealing direct to the angels themselves. I was about as afraid.

"What's your name, boy?" asked Matthew.

"Abney Gleaner."

"And where are you from?"

"New Karlsville. Or we were. It's gone now, overrun by a plague of the dead. That's why we come here. You're our only surviving kin, Mr. Scout," I was gabbling, trying to get my words to outpace my tears.

"Your father?"

"Robart Gleaner."

"Stepfather?"

"Old Gern Hollister."

The man drew back. He spoke hurriedly, we could only hear some of what was said. "It is my cousin . . . her boy . . . can we . . . there's . . ."

From the forest came a faraway roar.

By now a crowd of people from the fields had gathered around our back. Half of them were curious, the other half looking back over their shoulders at the woods.

"What happened to my cousin?" said Matthew.

"They roused the dragon!" shouted one. Murmurs went through this meager crowd, their hands tightened on their tools.

"Leave them be!" shouted Coppergather. "Let the boy answer!"

Quinn gritted his teeth and spoke for me. "She was bit in the hand. I took it off. She could be okay, if you open the gates. She needs help."

Coppergather shook his head regretfully. "We cannot let her in. The boy, yes, and you yourself knight may enter, but the woman cannot come within. Neither can she stay outside. She has the sickness, and must die."

My mom moaned again, shook her head jerkily. "No," she said. "No."

Painfully, she lifted her face up. Her chin was wet with thick saliva, her eyes crusted at the corners. The guards on the gate shouted at these signs of the sickness. The crowd behind us backed away.

"That you, Matthew?" she said. Her voice was a croak, every word cracked.

"I'm here."

"It's good to hear your voice again. Your letters have been a comfort."

"I am sorry I have not been able to write you for so long, but we have become cut off."

My mother laughed weakly. "So we see."

Matthew laughed with her, quietly though, appalled at what was occurring. "She's my kin alright," he said, more loudly this time. "For the love of Jesus, let her in!"

"We cannot let her in. She cannot stay. She is afflicted," said Coppergather. "Sir knight, my prior offer stands. Decide quickly, the dragon may come here."

Mom slipped from the horse. She'd already made her mind up then, I think, that she wasn't going inside. I don't know where she was trying to get to. Wherever it was, she didn't make it. She kneeled down, straight from standing. It must've hurt, falling on her knees like that, but her body was all knotted up and she couldn't get down no other way.

I ran to her side. She reached into her bodice with shaking hands and pulled out a neatly folded letter, then her purse, heavy with her bride price.

"T-t-take these. You . . . Safe here," she said. "Matthew is a good man."

Her face was puffy and pale, drenched with sweat. Gluey saliva had collected at the corners of her mouth.

The people of the wall looked on.

"Mrs. Hollister," said Quinn softly.

"You got us here. You'll get your money." She spoke through her teeth, pained and angry.

"It ain't about the money."

"I didn't mean . . ." she swallowed painfully. Her teeth ground. "The fever. The fury rising in me. The devil . . . He's taking me places I don't want to go."

"Mom! No."

"Look into my eyes."

She held up her face. The irises of her eyes, once a pretty hazel, were shot through with veins of clear blue. She was turning, my own mother becoming a monster.

"It won't be long until she's gone," said Quinn.

"Finish me. There isn't anything they can do. Before it's too late."

Quinn looked at me.

"Boy," he said steadily. "Go back to the horses and look away."

"Mom?" I said.

"Do as he says, Abney!" she roared at me, hardly coherent. It was the sickness talking. It always makes them rage before it takes their voices away forever.

"Mom!"

She tried to smile but it came out a snarl. Her teeth clacked, but she fought back the thing rising up in her and looked right at me. "You're a man now, Abney. You'll do fine, just fine, my baby, my son."

"Get to the horses," said Quinn.

I hesitated.

"Go, boy, now!"

"Abney, go! Can't . . . I can't . . ." Her head jerked.

I took a step back, but couldn't look away.

My mother's arms snapped hard to her sides. She lifted her head up and let out a long, screaming shout at the sky. It was the worst sound in the world, the sound of someone's soul dying. She tried to speak, but her mouth got stuck on the words, one particle of speech clicking in her throat over and over. "Ng, ng, ng, ng . . ."

"I have to do it now." Quinn's hand went to his gun. He looked at me, but I wasn't going anywhere. That made him sorry, I think. He couldn't do nothing but what he did next.

He drew his gun and pointed it at my mother's head. Her eyes were running with tears, mouth with spit. She was already losing what made her her. Her eyes rolled. She was panting, sharp, animal noises.

Quinn cocked his gun with his thumb.

"God keep you, Mrs. Hollister."

"My name," she grunted, "is Sarah."

The gun boomed out the end of my childhood.

That was the one time I saw Quinn use his gun.

My mother fell sideways into the dirt, blood pooling around her. Red shot through with gray and sticky black.

When I saw her dead like that, my mother, who had bore me and raised me and sacrificed everything in the end, then I knew what she said was true.

I was a man.

Blood Sacrifice

QUINN LEFT ME STARING at my mother's side. I couldn't take me eyes off her. Her face was locked in a savage grimace. The bullet hole in her forehead was neat as a stitch, the back of her head hollowed out by its exit. Pale brains spread over the dirt. I felt sick, my knees shook so hard I should have toppled over there and then. But I didn't, nor did I throw up. I just stood there. I couldn't take my eyes away. Such terrible power in the hand of one man. I became afraid of Quinn then. The boy that I was had been carried up by the stories I'd heard, the fact that he was a warrior of the angels. But though I never stopped liking or respecting him, the man I was becoming knew to fear him.

I heard Quinn shouting up to the castellan through a fog of grief, distant but clear.

"I have done as you asked."

"Show your seal, then we will let you within."

I didn't see the marvelous and awful angel trapped in the seal. All I saw was my mom's dead face, the mouth open, eyes halfway to unliving blue. I hoped it hadn't been too late, that her soul would find its way to heaven, and God would permit her bliss.

Quinn was calling me.

"Son!"

I lifted my head. It was heavy as lead.

"Come on."

"My mom . . ."

Coppergather shouted down. "We shall deal with the body. We have the correct rites, and a place of resting for all good Christian souls."

"She was a good soul," said Quinn. "See you treat her with respect."

The gates groaned outwards, and we were permitted inside. Five men in matching livery held us in the gate until Coppergather came down from the tower.

Coppergather had the same, hard way of looking at things that Quinn had. He shook Quinn's hand. "I am sorry about the woman." He looked at me. "There was no choice, boy."

I nodded, unable to speak. If I'd opened up my mouth, only tears would have come.

"These parts are not lightly traveled," said Coppergather to Quinn. "The dragon is a constant threat to us, and strange things dwell in the northern woods. We are few in number, and have barely enough land to feed ourselves. Some years ago, the dragon became more aggressive, taking our livestock from the edges of our fields, and our people from the woods. We do not look kindly upon strangers. Nevertheless, Matthew has agreed to take the boy in."

"Thank—" began Quinn. But Coppergather held up his hands.

"Delay your thanks, knight. Matthew's adoption of his kin is conditional."

"What are the conditions?" said Quinn.

"They are not for me to decide. You have roused the dragon. When this happens, there is always a price." Coppergather was deeply troubled. "We must see what Brother Amos has to say about it."

~

Two rows of armored men marched us across the courtyard of the fort. This was a true castle, entirely military in nature, another new sight for me. It was not like it is now, with many houses and workshops outside the walls and gardens in the ward. Then all of Winfort's industry was hidden inside, and nervous men kept constant watch from the battlement. The central square was much bigger back then. Where the hall and church are now were open spaces, marked out for sparring. Otherwise, you might recognize it. The granary is the same, the houses, weaver's row. But what was really different in my memory was the atmosphere. There was a sadness on the place, a resignation. There were few old people there, and hardly any children.

The keep was like it is now, tall and imposing, the great doors set high up the steps behind a drawbridge. The stone ditch was full of spikes then, not water. No fish swam there.

For the first time I entered the Winfort keep.

The main hall was a cool space all of stone. There was a dampness to it—there is, still. Huge fireplaces on two walls burned up six-foot logs, but they did little to drive off the chill. In that man-made cave, winter had come early.

Back then there was a wooden dais at the far side of the room; that's gone now. Upon that Lord Corn had his throne. More armed men flanked him, six to a side. Each was decked in mail reaching down to their knees, coats of metal lamellae over the tops, and padded leather underneath. They had shoulder guards and thick steel helmets with white horsehair plumes on their heads. They gripped the hilts of their swords with their right hands, ready to draw. They looked at Quinn through narrowed eyes. Until then, I had no idea that knights were not always welcome. Quinn was a hero to me.

Lord Corn was sickly when I came here, and soon

to die. He had been a great warrior, until weapons born from the old knowledge took his breath in the war. His skin was gray, his lips pale. I've been told he was powerfully muscled in his youth, but had become emaciated. He was swathed in wolf and smilodon furs, and yet still he seemed cold.

"A knight champion?" said Lord Corn. "I have not seen your kind in these parts since the war." He smiled. There was nothing but derision and pain in his expression. His teeth were too long in pale, shrunken gums. "And come up from the southwest. There is a dragon in these parts, surely you are aware?" Every word dripped with bitterness. "Or do you simply not care for yourself, or for the others that your passing through the dragon's lands jeopardizes?" Corn's anger brought on a hacking cough. A servant hurried to his side bearing a silver spittoon held in a cloth. Corn leant over the side of his throne and hawked and spat for a good half minute; stringy yellow mucous from deep in the lung, streaked with dark blood clots.

He groaned and leaned back into his throne. Corn's man fussed and dabbed at his lips. The lord waved him away angrily. The servant's cloth came away red.

"Gas," said Quinn.

Corn nodded. "I got a lungful of it in the war, not long before Columbus fell. I've been dying ever since. Twenty years of pain."

"You're still alive."

Corn's yellow eyes swiveled down. "I don't call this living. Many gifts I've been given by the angels. Land no one can farm. A dragon set on my doorstep to punish a dead emperor. A dragon that grows more wicked with every passing summer. And this weakness. So heavily I am blessed. Amos!" Corn attempted a shout. It came out wheezy, feeble.

Brother Amos wore the rough homespun of the mendicant order, the same robes I wear now. He was old, sinewy and dry as the corpse of a rat found mummified in a wainscot. He held his head forward of his body, like he was always trying to catch something someone was saying just out of earshot. He was blind, see, in both eyes. He told me, months later, that he had been all his life.

His blank white eyes stared at us both. When they fell on me, they bored through flesh and bone to look in on my soul, and I shriveled inside surely as a sinner shrivels in the fires of hell.

"A boy and a knight," he said. "And a dragon at our gates. What conundrums the lord sets us for our troubles."

The blind eyes fixed themselves on Quinn. He never failed to find the man he wished to address. Some say he was possessed of angel-given second sight, and he was feared for it.

"Did you fight in the war?" asked Amos. His voice was surprisingly strong from one so old and frail.

"I've fought in a lot of wars."

"Do not test me, knight, I ask in amity. Did you fight in the war of the emperor and the angels?"

"I did."

"You fought on the side of Pittsburgh."

"Against the angels of Columbus."

"We do our best to stay on good terms with those west of the river," said Corn. "Ohio has still not healed its hurts. Your arrival here is unwelcome."

"Don't see how my coming makes any odds to your situation."

"The angels see clearly and far," snapped Corn. "Their eyes are forever on their agents."

Quinn was not fazed. "Atlantis is a free city, unaffiliated with the league. The angels there do as they see fit, and I did what the angels asked. That business is all passed."

"You serve them no longer?" asked Amos.

"Pittsburgh's problem with Columbus is not my quarrel anymore."

"You speak as if the destruction of Columbus was not the end of it," said Amos.

"Affairs like that never end. They weren't the end of it

for the Emperor of Virginia. And you, living here under dragon-threat on the edge of the Wildlands? I reckon you know that too."

Lord Corn sneered. "These lands were gifted me for my part in the war. I am warden of the marches, beholden to neither kingdom. Our hold on the land is tenuous. We are dependent on the goodwill of Virginia and Ohio both. I will not risk my holdings here by antagonizing those west of the river. You must leave."

"Your name, sir?" asked Amos.

"I am Quinn."

Brother Amos cocked his head on one side. He remained so for a moment, then spoke rapidly. The effect was somewhat birdlike. "Jacob Quinn, sanctioned by the Angels of Atlantis as their warrior and their agent. Champion of the South, onetime general of the emperor. Hero of the Battle of Four Rivers."

Corn smiled. His pale lips gleamed with residual sputum. "Brother Amos has memorized the names and deeds of all the angels' knights recorded in the chronicle."

"You're a long way from home, sea knight," said Amos.

"I've a long way yet to go."

"You are the last knight of your city?"

"Far as I know. Not many knights left from anywhere these days."

Amos nodded. "A pity."

"We're not in fashion anymore," said Quinn. "Angels made us, used us, found us wanting. I'm a leftover, just trying to get by."

"You are not in fashion any longer," agreed Corn harshly. "Dragons and revenants and slithering things are the preferred tools of heaven upon the Earth in these times. The emperor has a lot to answer for. We are all punished for one man's ambition. I was rewarded for my service against him. See the bounty of the angels!" his dry voice whispered round the chilly hall.

Quinn shrugged. He unhitched his falchion's quillions from his longsword. The lord's men tensed as his hand touched the hilts.

"Treachery is poorly rewarded, even by those it serves," said Quinn.

Lord Corn's face set in a mask, all hard angles of hate. He leaned forward on his throne, grunting with the effort. He raised a shaking hand and pointed at Quinn. "And we are now to be punished for another's thoughtlessness." Corn's jaundiced eyes came to rest on me. They were as cold and inimical as the eyes of the unliving.

Men stepped into the hall behind us. They carried crossbows, and they were all pointed at us.

"Remove the knight's weapons."

Quinn looked behind him questioningly. Castellan

Coppergather shook his head slightly.

The lord's guard came down from the steps, circling Quinn warily. Quinn took the measure of each, then raised his hands.

"I don't want any trouble with you here."

"By rights, I should slaughter you like a dog, Sir Quinn," spat Corn. "You and yours were on the side of the emperor, and his name is reviled here."

"I served the emperor at the behest of the angels. They are my masters."

Corn coughed once, hard. "And that is why I am forced to set you free." A jerk of Corn's chin, and Quinn's weapons belts were unbuckled.

"Your weapons will be returned at the gates. You will ride from here immediately."

"It ain't going to happen that way," said Quinn. He looked upward. "As God is my witness, I demand trial by combat, as is my right."

"Ha! Your conditions?"

"Should I win, this boy is to go free with no taint upon his character, that he be allowed to freely live within this community, the goods and monies he carries to remain with him, and that I be released with all my trappings and possessions, and allowed to proceed upon my journey unmolested. Those are my conditions."

Lord Corn snorted. "Petty concerns! There is a

dragon at the gate. You are free to go already. I deny your request."

"You cannot. Deny a trial and you defy the angels. My authority as their agent stands."

"When other matters are more pressing, I can do as I will. Let the angels judge me harshly if I am wrong. Remove him!"

Quinn shrugged off the men when they reached for his shoulders. "What about the boy?"

"The dragon has been roused. Only blood offering will send it back to sleep," said Amos. "You woke it." He was apologetic.

"You're going to give the boy to the dragon?"

Men closed in on me, blocking my way out.

"Do you propose that I sacrifice one of my own to save this stranger? Is that it, one of my people should offer themselves up in his place? You think so, very well!" Lord Corn looked around the room. "Does anyone of you volunteer to take the place of this boy?"

Cousin Matthew stepped forward, but he was grabbed and pulled back into position. He looked at me in dismay.

"So be it," said brother Amos sorrowfully. "Sound the horns. Let the beast know we have an offering, and we shall pray that it is enough to spare us from its wrath. Take the boy to the stone."

"Quinn!" I cried.

Quinn tensed.

"Make a move to aid him and I will have you shot down," Corn warned.

Quinn relaxed. This time, he accepted the hands of Corn's warriors on his shoulders.

Corn smiled. "Sensible. Go. Do not return."

"Quinn!" I kicked and struggled as the men dragged me away, but I couldn't get free of them.

"I'm sorry, son," said Quinn. "I'm sorry."

~

They kept me prisoner overnight while horns blew over and over again, inviting the dragon to dinner. The sound of people coming into the castle went on late into the night as the valley was emptied. A pair of women attended me. They were not unkind, they fed me and helped me wash, but did not speak much. I heard my cousin arguing with the guards after dark, but he was sent away and I did not see him again until it was all over.

Morning came. I had not slept. You might think I cried, but I didn't. I spent the night staring at the roughness of my cell wall.

They took me out into a chilly morning awash with pale sunlight.

Quinn had gone. There was no sign of him or his horses as the gates opened and I was taken out into the fields and to that terrible stone. The betrayal hit me more than the notion that I was about to die.

My guards held my unresisting hands in place and screwed the manacles shut. The metal was cold with the night, and hurt my flesh. They fit just fine. They favored women and children for their sacrifices in those times, or I could've just slipped my hand right out. That made me hate them for a long while afterwards. One of the guards wouldn't look at me. The other gave me a grim look. Not hateful or anything of that kind, but sympathetic.

"Keep your eyes closed, boy," he said. "Don't look at it. It'll be over quickly."

They withdrew fast, the castle gates creaking shut behind them. People lined the battlement, looking down on me, all solemn. For hours there was no sign of the dragon. The sun grew hot, the stone stayed cool at my back. Those hours are burned so deep into my memory they've become a part of me in a way most memories don't. But they're outside of me at the same time, a little eternity of suffering separate and complete in its right. The flags hung limp on the castle towers. There was a hush over the vale, not a human word was spoken, no bird sang in the forest crowding the fields.

Finally a roar came forth from the west, and the priest

came up onto the tallest tower in answer. Amos mounted a platform there. It rose over the crenellations on the wall, with a lectern at the front. Damn thing was a pulpit, and he was going to preach. His apologetic nature had bled away in the dark. That morning he was all righteousness. Strangely, I never hated him for that. He was doing the Lord God's work, and the bidding of his prince. He and I became friends, eventually.

"These strangers have come into our rightful lands!" he said. "These territories granted to our Lord Corn by God's own angels. They have roused the guardian of the river against us, and his wrath is hot and dire. We call upon you, dragon of the angels, take this interloper so that we might live with you in peace. Let the Lord's will be done!"

The priest stepped down from his platform, retreating with the rest to the safety of stone. The inhabitants of the Winfort peeked out at me between the teeth of the walls.

They didn't have long to wait.

A terrifying smashing sound came through the brush behind me. The worst of it was that I couldn't see behind me on account of that tall stone. I twisted in the chains, the manacles biting the skin round my wrists, but the stone at my back kept me from seeing. Branches broke. The dragon came out of the woods. I heard its heavy tread in the field, the grind of rocks pressed into one another by great weight, and a reptilian slithering.

I looked up at the cloudless sky and prayed harder than I've ever prayed in my life, before or since.

The dragon's footfalls came closer, a slow prowl. If you could hear a cat walk, I imagine it would sound like that. A vibrating, throaty breathing came with it, deep and gusty as a forge bellows. A sense of malice gripped me, and I pissed myself with the fear of it. The prayer died on my lips, and I started to moan. You think I'm a coward, and that you would do better? I know that ain't so.

The dragon spoke, a wash of heat rolling from it with every word.

"I hear thy call, priest," rumbled the dragon. "Thou hast angered me. My territory has been subject to vile trespass. This insult I shall not brook."

"We are contrite, servant of the servants of the Lord. Do you accept our offering?"

The dragon breathed in.

A movement at the corner of my eye. A silver tentacle made of metal segments and tipped with a glowing, red glass eye slid around the rock. The eye glowed dimly, flaring when it fixed upon me. It looked at my face, dipped down to survey the rest of my body. The tentacle reared up, as some snakes are wont to do before a strike, then it slipped away behind the rock.

"A petty morsel, and not of your own. This stranger has little value to you, and therefore none to me. Where are your daughters, where are your maidens?"

"Do you accept our offering and our contrition?" shouted out Brother Amos.

The dragon roared, my ears rang with it, and I screamed. I was crying now, sobbing great wet tears. "I'm sorry God, I'm sorry Jesus," over and over in my mind. I tried to say it, but nothing but moaning would come.

"This thy morsel I accept, priest, but I bring you people of the castle warning—trouble ye my lands again, and a greater tithe in blood and flesh shall I demand! Offer one from outside thy flock again and thy priestly skin I will devour!"

None said ought to the creature, but watched in abject terror from the castle. Such was the sense of evil I had of this thing behind me that I reckoned the castle walls to be no defense against it at all. This was the wrath of the Lord clothed in flesh. I could feel that without seeing it.

It paced around rock, that rumbling breath growing loud. I screwed my eyes tight shut. I didn't want to see it. The heat coming off the thing hit me hard, furnace heat, not quite enough to burn but not far off.

"Look upon me, child," it said.

I turned my head to the side.

"Look upon my majesty and fear me!"

There must've been some spark of defiance in me under all that terror, because I refused.

It roared again. I cried out at the pain in my ears. It backed up, because the heat got less. There was a sound like the wind, a sucking in of air, and a tremendous whining noise.

I was going to die, burned up by a dragon's flame.

Another sound came to me, penetrating the ringing in my ears. The galloping of hooves, the skid of a horse coming to a rapid halt.

"Hold! Hold!" came a voice.

"Quinn?" I said. My voice was real weak, barely a whisper.

"I am Quinn, Knight of Atlantis. Begone from this place! Leave the boy! I command you by the authority of the angels!"

The whining stopped. The dragon retreated from me. I opened my eyes.

I've never seen anything like it, not even in my nightmares. Think you know what a dragon looks like? Think again. Think you'd see scales, and claws, and a snout like an alligator? Wings and frills and all that? None of it.

Part of it was animal, thick legs dense with muscle, heavy feet tipped with three silver claws. But at God's command the devil had given it a thick suit of armor of shining metal, moonbright and glorious. The plates of it were cleverly made, sliding over each other without a sound. This harness sat on its hips and shoulders, clad the lower parts of all four legs, covered its belly and its spine. There were anchoring plates to which the rest attached, and they grew right from its body, knurling the skin where it grew over the metal. What flesh I could see was leathery and dark, gray-brown, thick as a mastodon's, free of scales and furless.

A long scorpion's tail tipped with a scimitar blade arched over its back. There were wings, flexing bat things like in the stories. Dense and leathery skin webbed silver fingers sharp as needles, but I don't think it could fly. Six limbs, just like a dragon. In every other respect it was nothing like any picture I have ever seen.

Where its neck and head should have been was a crop of thrashing tendrils, twenty of them, forged of banded steel in the workshops of hell. A red eye of glass tipped each one. There was an opening beneath that, a mouth of sorts, lined with hooked teeth. From this vented spurts of blue and green infernal fire that burned everything it lit upon, be it rock or flesh.

How it ate, how it lived or bred, I could not say. This was a creature of Satan himself, coughed up from the pits of hell to ruin the lands of men. God's judgment on the sons of Adam for his perfidy and pride. Heed the good book, listen to your pastor. God watches us always, and he has no mercy for sinners in this life.

"A knight? A knight! One servant seeks to command the other. See thou that I am mightier. Begone or burn in my fires," the dragon laughed; a harsh, diabolical racket.

"Release him. I command you!" shouted Quinn.

Quinn's horse reared and whinnied and Quinn raised his arm. In his upheld hand light flashed pure and silver. The image of the seal leapt up and out, magnified many times over but just as perfect as before. The angel with a bowed, cowled head, wings spread wide. The four ships, sails billowing, began their track around it.

"I do not answer to the angels of the ocean. Thy kind's day is done. Go back to wherever thou hast hidden thyself these last and sorry years, and leave me to my meal."

"I have the right of passage through all the angel's lands. Your fury is unjust."

"And the twain that rode with thee, sir knight? Who are these trespassers? Where is their token of passage?"

"They rode under my protection."

"None might pass these lands. They are under the view of the angels. I am their eyes and the might of their arm. Their punishment is upon this land. I am the curse of pride."

"The boy is innocent of any crime. He has no pride."

"He is a son of Adam. All are tainted by sin. He will suffer for the emperor's misdeeds, as all should suffer."

"I will not quit the field."

"Then thou art doomed."

The dragon's whining roar began again, and it took into itself a great draft of breath. It leaned backward, bunching up the chest and the mouth set there.

The dragon lunged forward, and a jet of brilliant flame roared from its slotlike mouth.

Quinn spurred Parsifal, and the great white horse leapt off the road. The dragon turned, chasing the knight and his steed with his fire. Straw and grass and everything the fire touched on burst into flame. The ground steamed. Stone shattered under its caress.

Quinn flashed by me, and I saw there was something attached to his belt, a crushed mass of gray metal strips.

The dragon's fire ceased. Quinn galloped around the back of the judging stone. Parsifal's hooves thundered on stripped fields, drawing away, but I couldn't credit that he'd abandon me for real.

The dragon's eye stalks swayed, and turned as one to glare at me.

"If thou art the one he would release, then thou shalt die immediately," said the dragon. "Let that settle our contest."

It came toward me. The eye stalks parted, and I saw in their midst a second mouth set within a fold of flesh. It thrust forward, like the head of a turtle but eyeless and bald. Cruel, interlocking teeth parted, exposing a cavernous throat.

Hooves drummed again. Quinn came in fast from the right, his lance now in his hand. The dragon, intent upon me, turned too late to avoid the knight. The tip of Quinn's lance pierced the creature's flank, sliding neatly between plates of armor. The tip penetrated a good arm's length before the lance shivered into pieces. The creature bellowed in anger and pain, and turned swiftly. It swiped with a heavy forelimb. Parsifal reared, and was knocked over. Quinn fell from the saddle and rolled free. Parsifal staggered up to his feet and ran, his eyes rolling with terror. Quinn was unhorsed, and at the dragon's mercy.

I could do nothing as I watched these two agents of the angels battle one another. Why would God release evil upon us, you might ask. The answer is that all punishment is by nature evil, and the greater the punishment required, the greater the evil inflicted. And the dragon, well, he was a great punishment indeed.

Quinn took out his longsword. The dragon swiped at him with a crushing paw. Quinn dodged. If he were to block such a blow it would achieve nothing, his sword would break or be driven back onto him, and he would surely die. He danced backwards in a low crouch as the dragon's stabbing tail slammed into the ground twice. The dragon howled in anger.

"Thou defiest me in my own land. For that you will die, agent of the Dreaming Cities or not."

The dragon drew in its breath once more, preparing to incinerate the knight. Quinn stood his ground as the whining of the inhalation built, lifting the crumpled mass of metal from his belt. He passed his longsword to his left hand, and held the ball ready in his right.

I found my voice. "Quinn! Look out!" I could not understand why he did not move!

The dragon released its fires. A cone of white heat blasted out toward the knight. Quinn leapt to the side, and ran directly toward the dragon, right alongside the borders of the creature's flame. He stood the heat, but not without injury. The dragon lumbered round, trying to catch Quinn in its breath. Quinn stayed always outside it.

I screamed. The dragon's fire was sweeping inexorably toward me as Quinn dashed at the beast.

In four strides Quinn came within a spear's length of the dragon's mouth. He drew back his arm, and threw the ball of metal into the heart of the inferno, then dived aside.

The dragon screamed. A hideous noise, loud and potent with misery. The fires shut off. The dragon curled in on itself and writhed upon the floor. Sparks and fire shot from the joints of its armor. Several of its eye stalks fell limp, the lights in the red eyes dying. It screamed and screamed, a weird crackling and popping coming from within its gut.

Quinn walked toward it. The dragon's eyes danced, and the beast tried to rise, but it flopped back down with a rattling moan of agony. Quinn sidestepped the flailing tail, kicked aside an enfeebled paw and drew back his sword. With a turn of his hand he thrust the blade deep into the nest of tentacles above the creature's upper mouth. With another smooth motion, he twisted and withdrew his blade. Thick vapors boiled off black blood that coated the sword end to end.

The dragon let out a hiccupping sob. The eye tentacles rattled against one another, and fell limp. The lights went out in all of them. The dragon drew in two slow breaths and lay still. The glow in its lower mouth flickered out. Its fires died, and its heat began to diminish.

Quinn turned to me. His threw down his longsword onto the smoking grass, and drew out his falchion as he strode toward me.

"Close your eyes," he said.

In my terror, I thought he meant to kill me.

"I ain't gonna hurt you! Turn your head! Close your eyes!"

He struck through one chain, a blow no normal man could make. In a shower of yellow sparks the chain parted.

"Your edge," I said stupidly.

Quinn gave me that quirk-mouthed look. The side of his face was raw and blistered. The secondhand heat of the dragon radiated off him. I'm pretty sure none but a knight could have withstood that temperature. A normal man would have cooked in his armor. "Damn the edge, son. I'm making a point."

He pushed my head to one side. "Close your eyes again."

Another chop and the second chain parted. I was free, and the dragon was dead.

Quinn Departs

FROM THE EAST, the south, the north and northwest, the eyes of the angels gathered thickly, twenty or more of them, all in different heraldry and form. Miniature angels flew alongside strange machines and eagles with mechanical heads. Whatever their shape, they were of the same purpose, spies of the Dreaming Cities, and they gathered over the dragon like buzzards.

"They've come to mourn the dragon," I said.

Quinn nodded. He rode Parsifal, Clemente clopping along behind. I walked with him, jogging a little to keep up.

"Will they punish us for its death?"

"I killed it. Angels won't risk another war among themselves over that. Their rules mean something, leastaways where their own affairs are concerned." Quinn's face had healed unnaturally fast. But for a faint reddening on his right side, his hurts had all disappeared.

We fell quiet. We didn't have much to say to one another. I was safe, he was leaving.

"How did you kill it?" I asked at last.

"Lead strips," he said. "Those in the Gone Before used them on their houses. I was gone awhile because I had to find them. Bundle them up, toss them in. The dragon's fire melted it." He smiled in a small and private way. "Lead is a real good conductor of electricity. Once it got into the innards that's that. No more dragon."

"I don't understand."

Quinn shrugged. "Dragon runs off electricity. Most things do, even you and I in part."

I still didn't understand. Even now, I don't.

"Thank you, Mr. Quinn."

"You ain't got nothing to thank me for, boy," he said. "I'm sorry about your mother. I tried my best." He tossed my mother's purse down at me. It was much heavier than it should have been.

I opened it. "You've returned too much!" I said. "Half of this was for you," I said. I held it up to him.

"I didn't hold up my end of the bargain, so there's no need for you to. I took half of what we agreed, that leaves you three-quarters of your mother's bride price. The fee for one person delivered safely. I'd give you it all, but even a knight needs money. Keep it close by you, don't be tempted to spend it. You might need it one day."

"Where are you going?"

"Like I said, I'm headed for Columbus."

"But there ain't nothing but plains of glass there," I

said, echoing the postmaster's words.

"There's always more to something than what's on the surface."

The road broadened out. It disappeared into the forest at the far end of the valley, the beginning of the Northern Wildlands.

"Quinn?"

"Yes?"

"Why are you going all the way out there?"

"I got business there. Unfinished business. I'm looking for someone, son."

"Who? Is it your oath, your badge? What happened, Quinn?"

He reined Parsifal in, bringing the horse to a sharp stop. He frowned down on me. Dust curled around us.

"You gotta learn when a man's done giving answers."

"But . . ." I stopped. I didn't know what I was saying. Knowing what he was doing wasn't the important thing. What was important was that I didn't want him to go. A dozen overlapping notions made up my yearning. He was the last connection to my mother; he'd saved me from a dragon. I was safe with him, and now he was abandoning me for real.

I felt sorry for him, yeah, that too. He didn't have anybody. I could've been somebody to keep him company.

I couldn't say any of that, and if he sensed even a part

of it, I couldn't see it in his face.

"Son," he said more kindly. "I don't like no one knowing my business. I prefer to keep it that way. I've told you more than I tell most, be content with that."

He clicked his tongue and urged Parsifal into a quick walk, leaving me behind. But then he stopped and turned back to look at me one last time, this knight. He was the closest thing I'll ever get to meeting an angel. Closest thing I'll ever get to God, in this life anyways. He smiled but his eyes were sad, and I wondered if God smiled like that—sorry for the creation he had made. "Stay safe, Abney. The world's a terrible place, it needs more people in it with good hearts."

"Quinn!" I shouted.

The knight wheeled his horse around.

"Hyah!" he said, digging in his heels. Parsifal set up a gentle canter, not too fast for his smaller companion to keep pace, but fast enough. Within a few minutes Quinn had reached the end of the valley, and then he was gone into the trees. I watched the empty road for minutes. Dust hung on the morning, flour white.

That time, when he left, that was the only time he ever used my name.

I never saw him again.

Reluctantly, I turned my back on Quinn's road, and made for the castle, Winfort, this place. After the dragon

was killed, they let me stay, and it became my home. Matthew raised me, as good as he could. He was a kind man. Amos taught me. I tried to get a wife, but none would have me, so I became a priest. Not long after that, Amos died.

And I'm still here, aren't I?

The sun treated us to a crisp fall evening as it fell by degree toward the west. In that clear light, the angels' eyes flocking around the dragon's corpse danced round one final time. They were speaking. "Quinn, Quinn, Quinn," they said, a sad music. Blue light played from them across the dragon's corpse, and the thing just faded out of existence, vanished like mist under a strong sun. The eyes of the angels soared away, each in a different direction.

~

So what's the point of all this, you young ones might think. The mumblings of an old man whose time has run out, you'll be thinking. Well they ain't.

The point of this goes so: you think you can find a place to mind your own business, to raise your crops and your family. That if you choose your spot well, and the Lord smiles on you, then you can live your life free of the meddling of mighty men like the emperor.

That just ain't the case. Minding your own business is not a choice open to us. No matter how you try, no matter where you hide, what great men does affects you. Twenty years after the emperor roused the wrath of the Pittsburgh angels, the plague of dead they unleashed wiped New Karlsville off the face of the Earth. Twenty years on! What our fault was in that, I cannot say. Think on this too—the angels gave land to Lord Corn, and then put a dragon on his doorstep. They said they were punishing another man, the emperor. It never looked that way to Corn, and it don't look that way to me.

Angels aren't to be trusted. But that don't mean that they are evil. I'll tell you why. Remember this. If the Lord moves mysteriously against you, and at times his doings seem unfair, then remember that no man is without sin. Not you, nor I, nor the highest lord or the lowliest farmer.

Not the knights either.

And that includes Quinn.

Time's getting on for me now. I reckon this here will be one of the last times I tell of how I came to Winfort, met a knight, and survived a dragon. The story of my life is nearly done. I got a winter left in me, maybe two. Here I bow out. I can't say I'm sorry. Pain's a terrible good friend to a man my age. He's outstayed his welcome, and I'd dearly like to see the back of him. I've watched things

get better for folks. No man can ask for more than to see his people prosper, and so I'll go to the good Lord with a light heart.

The likes of Quinn though, their stories never end. Heroes don't ever die. I know that, out there, Quinn carried on his search. Who was he looking for, I don't know. It bothered me for years that I never found out, but I guess I've made my peace with that. Maybe he found him, maybe he didn't. Whatever fortune did to Quinn, wherever he went, and why, I'm sure as the good Lord is enthroned in heaven that someone, somewhere knows what happened to Quinn next. And if one of you young ones grows up, and goes out from Winfort, up toward where Columbus was and now there's only glass, someone, somewhere might tell you. I sure hope they do. If you find out, stop by my grave and whisper it to the earth when you come home, it'd be much appreciated.

The story of Quinn ain't over yet, not by a long chalk.

About the Author

GUY HALEY is the former deputy editor of *SFX* magazine and the former editor of *Death Ray* and Games Workshop's *White Dwarf*. He lives in Yorkshire with his wife and son, where he now spends his time writing novels full time.

guyhaley.wordpress.com

TOR·COM

Science fiction. Fantasy. The universe.

And related subjects.

*

More than just a publisher's website, *Tor.com*
is a venue for **original fiction, comics,** and
discussion of the entire field of SF and fantasy,
in all media and from all sources. Visit our site
today—and join the conversation yourself.

CPSIA information can be obtained
at www.ICGtesting.com
Printed in the USA
FSOW02n1536280416
19805FS